Janet casts the Flaming Sword into the Well

MORE ENGLISH FAIRY TALES

Collected and Edited by

JOSEPH JACOBS

Editor of "Folk-Lore"

Illustrated by

JOHN D. BATTEN

G.P. Putnam's Sons
New York and London

*YOU KNOW HOW
TO GET INTO THIS BOOK*

*Knock at the Knocker on the Door,
Pull the Bell at the side.*

*Then, if you are very quiet, you will hear
a teeny tiny voice say through the grating
"Take down the Key." This you will find at the
back: you cannot mistake it, for it has J.J.
in the wards. Put the Key in the Keyhole, which
it fits exactly, unlock the door, and*

WALK IN

Fourteenth Impression

To

MY SON SYDNEY

ÆTAT. XIII

Preface

This volume will come, I fancy, as a surprise both to my brother folk-lorists and to the public in general. It might naturally have been thought that my former volume (*English Fairy Tales*) had almost exhausted the scanty remains of the traditional folk-tales of England. Yet I shall be much disappointed if the present collection is not found to surpass the former in interest and vivacity, while for the most part it goes over hitherto untrodden ground, the majority of the tales in this book have either never appeared before, or have never been brought between the same boards.

In putting these tales together, I have acted on the same principles as in the preceding volume, which has already, I am happy to say, established itself as a kind of English Grimm. I have taken English tales wherever I could find them, one from the United States, some from the Lowland Scotch, and a few have been adapted from ballads, while I have left a couple in their original metrical form. I have rewritten most of them, and in doing so have adopted the traditional English style of folk-telling, with its "Wells" and "Lawkamercy" and archaic touches, which are known nowadays as vulgarisms. From former experience, I find that each of these principles has met with some dissent from critics who have written from the high and lofty standpoint of folk-lore, or from the lowlier vantage of "mere literature." I take this occasion to soften their ire, or perhaps give them further cause for reviling.

My folk-lore friends look on with sadness while they view me laying profane hands on the sacred text of my originals. I have actually at times introduced or deleted whole incidents, have given another turn to a tale, or finished off one that was incomplete, while I have had no scruple in prosing a ballad or softening down over-abundant dialect. This is rank sacrilege in the eyes of the rigid orthodox in matters folk-lorical. My defence might be that I had a cause at heart as sacred as our science of folk-lore—the filling of our children's imaginations with bright trains of images. But even on the lofty heights of folk-lore science I am not entirely defenceless. Do my friendly critics believe that even Campbell's materials had not been modified by the various narrators before they reached the great J.F.? Why may I not have the same privilege as any other story-teller, especially when I know the ways of story-telling as she is told in English, at least as well as a Devonshire or Lancashire peasant? And—conclusive argument—wilt thou, oh orthodox brother folk-lorist, still continue to use Grimm and Asbjörnsen? Well, they did the same as I.

Then as to using tales in Lowland Scotch, whereat a Saturday Reviewer, whose identity and fatherland were not difficult to guess, was so shocked. Scots a dialect of English! Scots tales the same as English! Horror and Philistinism! was the Reviewer's outcry. Matter of fact is my reply, which will only confirm him, I fear, in his convictions. Yet I appeal to him, why make a difference between tales told on different sides of the Border? A tale told in Durham or Cumberland in a dialect which only Dr. Murray could distinguish from Lowland Scotch, would on all hands be allowed to be "English." The same tale told a few miles farther North, why should we refuse it the same qualification? A tale in Henderson is English: why not a tale in Chambers, the majority of whose tales are to be found also south of the Tweed?

The truth is, my folk-lore friends and my Saturday Reviewer differ with me on the important problem of the origin of folk-tales. They think that a tale probably originated where it was found. They therefore attribute more importance than I to the exact form in which it is found and restrict it to the locality of birth. I consider the probability to lie in an origin elsewhere: I think it more likely than not that any tale found in a place was rather brought there than born there. I have discussed this matter elsewhere[1] with all the solemnity its importance deserves, and cannot attempt further to defend my position here. But even the reader innocent of folk-lore can see that, holding these views, I do not attribute much anthropological value to tales whose origin is probably foreign, and am certainly not likely to make a hard-and-fast division between tales of the North Countrie and those told across the Border.

As to how English folk-tales should be told authorities also differ. I am inclined to follow the tradition of my old nurse, who was not bred at Girton and who scorned at times the rules of Lindley Murray and the diction of smart society. I have been recommended to adopt a diction not too remote from that of the Authorised Version. Well, quite apart from memories of my old nurse, we have a certain number of tales actually taken down from the mouths of the people, and these are by no means in Authorised form; they even trench on the "vulgar"—*i.e.*, the archaic. Now there is just a touch of snobbery in objecting to these archaisms and calling them "vulgar." These tales have been told, if not from time immemorial, at least for several generations, in a special form which includes dialect and "vulgar" words. Why desert that form for one which the children cannot so easily follow with "thous" and "werts" and all the artificialities of pseudo-Elizabethan? Children are not likely to say "darter" for "daughter," or to ejaculate "Lawkamercyme" because they come across these forms in their folk-tales. They recognise the unusual forms while enjoying the fun of them. I have accordingly retained the archaisms and the old-world formulæ which go so well with the folk-tale.

In compiling the present collection I have drawn on the store of 140 tales with which I originally started; some of the best of these I reserved for this when making up the former one. That had necessarily to contain the old favourites *Jack the Giant Killer*, *Dick Whittington*, and the rest, which are often not so interesting or so well told as the less familiar ones buried in periodicals or folk-lore collections. But since the publication of *English Fairy Tales*, I have been specially fortunate in obtaining access to tales entirely new and exceptionally well told, which have been either published during the past three years or have been kindly placed at my disposal by folk-lore friends. Among these, the tales reported by Mrs. Balfour, with a thorough knowledge of the peasants' mind and mode of speech, are a veritable acquisition. I only regret that I have had to tone down so much of dialect in her versions. She has added to my indebtedness to her by sending me several tales which are entirely new and inedited. Mrs. Gomme comes only second in rank among my creditors for thanks which I can scarcely pay without becoming bankrupt in gratitude. Other friends have been equally kind, especially Mr. Alfred Nutt, who has helped by adapting some of the book versions, and by reading the proofs, while to the Councils of the American and English Folk-Lore Societies I have again to repeat my thanks for permission to use materials which first appeared in their publications. Finally, I have had Mr. Batten with me once again—what should I or other English children do without him?

JOSEPH JACOBS.

[1]

See "The Science of Folk Tales and the Problem of Diffusion" in *Transactions of the International Folk-Lore Congress*, 1891. Mr. Lang has honoured me with a rejoinder, which I regard as a palinode, in his Preface to Miss Roalfe Cox's volume of variants of *Cinderella* (Folk-Lore Society, 1892).

Contents

THE PIED PIPER OF FRANCHVILLE

HEREAFTERTHIS

THE GOLDEN BALL

MY OWN SELF

THE BLACK BULL OF NORROWAY

YALLERY BROWN

THREE FEATHERS

SIR GAMMER VANS

TOM HICKATHRIFT

THE HEDLEY KOW

GOBBORN SEER

LAWKAMERCYME

TATTERCOATS

THE WEE BANNOCK

JOHNNY GLOKE

COAT O' CLAY

THE THREE COWS

THE BLINDED GIANT

SCRAPEFOOT

THE PEDLAR OF SWAFFHAM

THE OLD WITCH

THE THREE WISHES

THE BURIED MOON

A SON OF ADAM

THE CHILDREN IN THE WOOD

THE HOBYAHS

A POTTLE O' BRAINS

THE KING OF ENGLAND AND HIS THREE SONS

KING JOHN AND THE ABBOT OF CANTERBURY

RUSHEN COATIE

THE KING 'O THE CATS

TAMLANE

THE STARS IN THE SKY

NEWS!

PUDDOCK, MOUSIE AND RATTON

THE LITTLE BULL-CALF

THE WEE, WEE MANNIE

HABETROT AND SCANTLIE MAB

OLD MOTHER WIGGLE-WAGGLE

CATSKIN

STUPID'S CRIES

THE LAMBTON WORM

THE WISE MEN OF GOTHAM

THE PRINCESS OF CANTERBURY

NOTES AND REFERENCES

MORE ENGLISH FAIRY TALES

The Pied Piper

Newtown, or Franchville, as 't was called of old, is a sleepy little town, as you all may know, upon the Solent shore. Sleepy as it is now, it was once noisy enough, and what made the noise was—rats. The place was so infested with them as to be scarce worth living in. There wasn't a barn or a corn-rick, a store-room or a cupboard, but they ate their way into it. Not a cheese but they gnawed it hollow, not a sugar puncheon but they cleared out. Why the very mead and beer in the barrels was not safe from them. They'd gnaw a hole in the top of the tun, and down would go one master rat's tail, and when he brought it up round would crowd all the friends and cousins, and each would have a suck at the tail.

Had they stopped here it might have been borne. But the squeaking and shrieking, the hurrying and scurrying, so that you could neither hear yourself speak nor get a wink of good honest sleep the live-long night! Not to mention that, Mamma must needs sit up, and keep watch and ward over baby's cradle, or there'd have been a big ugly rat running across the poor little fellow's face, and doing who knows what mischief.

Why didn't the good people of the town have cats? Well they did, and there was a fair stand-up fight, but in the end the rats were too many, and the pussies were regularly driven from the field. Poison, I hear you say? Why, they poisoned so many that it fairly bred a plague. Ratcatchers! Why there wasn't a ratcatcher from John o' Groat's house to the Land's End that hadn't tried his luck. But do what they might, cats or poison, terrier or traps, there seemed to be more rats than ever, and every day a fresh rat was cocking his tail or pricking his whiskers.

The Mayor and the town council were at their wits' end. As they were sitting one day in the town hall racking their poor brains, and bewailing their hard fate, who should run in but the town beadle. "Please your Honour," says he, "here is a very queer fellow come to town. I don't rightly know what to make of him." "Show him in," said the Mayor, and in he stepped. A queer fellow, truly. For there wasn't a colour of the rainbow but you might find it in some corner of his dress, and he was tall and thin, and had keen piercing eyes.

"I'm called the Pied Piper," he began. "And pray what might you be willing to pay me, if I rid you of every single rat in Franchville?"

Well, much as they feared the rats, they feared parting with their money more, and fain would they have higgled and haggled. But the Piper was not a man to stand nonsense, and the upshot was that fifty pounds were promised him (and it meant a lot of money in those old days) as soon as not a rat was left to squeak or scurry in Franchville.

Out of the hall stepped the Piper, and as he stepped he laid his pipe to his lips and a shrill keen tune sounded through street and house. And as each note pierced the air you might have seen a strange sight. For out of every hole the rats came tumbling. There were none too old and none too young, none too big and none too little to crowd at the Piper's heels and with eager feet and upturned noses to patter after him as he paced the streets. Nor was the Piper unmindful of the little toddling ones, for every fifty yards he'd stop and give an extra flourish on his pipe just to give them time to keep up with the older and stronger of the band.

Up Silver Street he went, and down Gold Street, and at the end of Gold Street is the harbour and the broad Solent beyond. And as he paced along, slowly and gravely, the townsfolk flocked to door and window, and many a blessing they called down upon his head.

As for getting near him there were too many rats. And now that he was at the water's edge he stepped into a boat, and not a rat, as he shoved off into deep water, piping shrilly all the while, but followed him, plashing, paddling, and wagging their tails with delight. On and on he played and played until the tide went down, and each master rat sank deeper and deeper in the slimy ooze of the harbour, until every mother's son of them was dead and smothered.

The tide rose again, and the Piper stepped on shore, but never a rat followed. You may fancy the townsfolk had been throwing up their caps and hurrahing and stopping up rat holes and setting the church bells a-ringing. But when the Piper stepped ashore and not so much as a single squeak was to be heard, the Mayor and the Council, and the townsfolk generally, began to hum and to ha and to shake their heads.

For the town money chest had been sadly emptied of late, and where was the fifty pounds to come from? Such an easy job, too! Just getting into a boat and playing a pipe! Why the Mayor himself could have done that if only he had thought of it.

So he hummed and ha'ad and at last, "Come, my good man," said he, "you see what poor folk we are; how can we manage to pay you fifty pounds? Will you not take twenty? When all is said and done, 't will be good pay for the trouble you've taken."

"Fifty pounds was what I bargained for," said the piper shortly; "and if I were you I'd pay it quickly. For I can pipe many kinds of tunes, as folk sometimes find to their cost."

"Would you threaten us, you strolling vagabond?" shrieked the Mayor, and at the same time he winked to the Council; "the rats are all dead and drowned," muttered he; and so "You may do your worst, my good man," and with that he turned short upon his heel.

"Very well," said the Piper, and he smiled a quiet smile. With that he laid his pipe to his lips afresh, but now there came forth no shrill notes, as it were, of scraping and gnawing, and squeaking and scurrying, but the tune was joyous and resonant, full of happy laughter and merry play. And as he paced down the streets the elders mocked, but from school-room and play-room, from nursery and workshop, not a child but ran out with eager glee and shout following gaily at the Piper's call. Dancing, laughing, joining hands and tripping feet, the bright throng moved along up Gold Street and down Silver Street, and beyond Silver Street lay the cool green forest full of old oaks and wide-spreading beeches. In and out among the oak-trees you might catch glimpses of the Piper's many-coloured coat. You might hear the laughter of the children break and fade and die away as deeper and deeper into the lone green wood the stranger went and the children followed.

All the while, the elders watched and waited. They mocked no longer now. And watch and wait as they might, never did they set their eyes again upon the Piper in his parti-coloured coat. Never were their hearts gladdened by the song and dance of the children issuing forth from amongst the ancient oaks of the forest.

Hereafterthis

Once upon a time there was a farmer called Jan, and he lived all alone by himself in a little farmhouse.

By-and-by he thought that he would like to have a wife to keep it all vitty for him.

So he went a-courting a fine maid, and he said to her: "Will you marry me?"

"That I will, to be sure," said she.

So they went to church, and were wed. After the wedding was over, she got up on his horse behind him, and he brought her home. And they lived as happy as the day was long.

One day, Jan said to his wife, "Wife can you milk-y?"

"Oh, yes, Jan, I can milk-y. Mother used to milk-y, when I lived home."

So he went to market and bought her ten red cows. All went well till one day when she had driven them to the pond to drink, she thought they did not drink fast enough. So she drove them right into the pond to make them drink faster, and they were all drowned.

When Jan came home, she up and told him what she had done, and he said, "Oh, well, there, never mind, my dear, better luck next time."

So they went on for a bit, and then, one day, Jan said to his wife, "Wife can you serve pigs?"

"Oh, yes, Jan, I can serve pigs. Mother used to serve pigs when I lived home."

So Jan went to market and bought her some pigs. All went well till one day, when she had put their food into the trough she thought they did not eat fast enough, and she pushed their heads into the trough to make them eat faster, and they were all choked.

When Jan came home, she up and told him what she had done, and he said, "Oh, well, there, never mind, my dear, better luck next time."

So they went on for a bit, and then, one day, Jan said to his wife, "Wife can you bake-y?"

"Oh, yes, Jan, I can bake-y. Mother used to bake-y when I lived home."

So he bought everything for his wife so that she could bake bread. All went well for a bit, till one day, she thought she would bake white bread for a treat for Jan. So she carried her meal to the top of a high hill, and let the wind blow on it, for she thought to herself that the wind would blow out all the bran. But the wind blew away meal and bran and all—so there was an end of it.

When Jan came home, she up and told him what she had done, and he said, "Oh, well, there, never mind, my dear, better luck next time."

So they went on for a bit, and then, one day, Jan said to his wife, "Wife can you brew-y?"

"Oh, yes, Jan, I can brew-y. Mother used to brew-y when I lived home."

So he bought everything proper for his wife to brew ale with. All went well for a bit, till one day when she had brewed her ale and put it in the barrel, a big black dog came in and looked up in her face. She drove him out of the house, but he stayed outside the door and still looked up in her face. And she got so angry that she pulled out the plug of the barrel, threw it at the dog, and said, "What dost look at me for? I be Jan's wife." Then the dog ran down the road, and she ran after him to chase him right away. When she came back again, she found that the ale had all run out of the barrel, and so there was an end of it.

When Jan came home, she up and told him what she had done, and he said, "Oh well, there, never mind, my dear, better luck next time."

So they went on for a bit, and then, one day, she thought to herself, "'T is time to clean up my house." When she was taking down her big bed she found a bag of groats on the tester. So when Jan came home, she up and said to him, "Jan, what is that bag of groats on the tester for?"

"That is for Hereafterthis, my dear."

Now, there was a robber outside the window, and he heard what Jan said. Next day, he waited till Jan had gone to market, and then he came and knocked at the door. "What do you please to want?" said Mally.

"I am Hereafterthis," said the robber, "I have come for the bag of groats."

Now the robber was dressed like a fine gentleman, so she thought to herself it was very kind of so fine a man to come for the bag of groats, so she ran upstairs and fetched the bag of groats, and gave it to the robber and he went away with it.

When Jan came home, she said to him, "Jan, Hereafterthis has been for the bag of groats."

"What do you mean, wife?" said Jan.

So she up and told him, and he said, "Then I'm a ruined man, for that money was to pay our rent with. The only thing we can do is to roam the world over till we find the bag of groats." Then Jan took the house-door off its hinges, "That's all we shall have to lie on," he said. So Jan put the door on his back, and they both set out to look for Hereafterthis. Many a long day they went, and in the night Jan used to put the door on the branches of a tree, and they would sleep on it. One night they came to a big hill, and there was a high tree at the foot. So Jan put the door up in it, and they got up in the tree and went to sleep. By-and-by Jan's wife heard a noise, and she looked to see what it was. It was an opening of a door in the side of the hill. Out came two gentlemen with a long table, and behind them fine ladies and gentlemen, each carrying a bag, and one of them was Hereafterthis with the bag of groats. They sat round the table, and began to drink and talk and count up all the money in the bags. So then Jan's wife woke him up, and asked what they should do.

"Now's our time," said Jan, and he pushed the door off the branches, and it fell right in the very middle of the table, and frightened the robbers so that they all ran away. Then Jan and his wife got down from the tree, took as many money-bags as they could carry on the door, and went straight home. And Jan bought his wife more cows, and more pigs, and they lived happy ever after.

The Golden Ball

There were two lasses, daughters of one mother, and as they came from the fair, they saw a right bonny young man stand at the house-door before them. They never saw such a bonny man before. He had gold on his cap, gold on his finger, gold on his neck, a red gold watch-chain—eh! but he had brass. He had a golden ball in each hand. He gave a ball to each lass, and she was to keep it, and if she lost it, she was to be hanged. One of the lasses, 't was the youngest, lost her ball. I'll tell thee how. She was by a park-paling, and she was tossing her ball, and it went up, and up, and up, till it went fair over the paling; and when she climbed up to look, the ball ran along the green grass, and it went right forward to the door of the house, and the ball went in and she saw it no more.

So she was taken away to be hanged by the neck till she was dead because she'd lost her ball.

But she had a sweetheart, and he said he would go and get the ball. So he went to the park-gate, but 't was shut; so he climbed the hedge, and when he got to the top of the hedge, an old woman rose up out of the dyke before him, and said, if he wanted to get the ball, he must sleep three nights in the house. He said he would.

Then he went into the house, and looked for the ball, but could not find it. Night came on and he heard bogles move in the courtyard; so he looked out o' the window, and the yard was full of them.

Presently he heard steps coming upstairs. He hid behind the door, and was as still as a mouse. Then in came a big giant five times as tall as he, and the giant looked round but did not see the lad, so he went to the window and bowed to look out; and as he bowed on his elbows to see the bogles in the yard, the lad stepped behind him, and with one blow of his sword he cut him in twain, so that the top part of him fell in the yard, and the bottom part stood looking out of the window.

There was a great cry from the bogles when they saw half the giant come tumbling down to them, and they called out, "There comes half our master, give us the other half."

So the lad said, "It's no use of thee, thou pair of legs, standing alone at the window, as thou hast no eye to see with, so go join thy brother;" and he cast the lower part of the giant after the top part. Now when the bogles had gotten all the giant they were quiet.

Next night the lad was at the house again, and now a second giant came in at the door, and as he came in the lad cut him in twain, but the legs walked on to the chimney and went up them. "Go, get thee after thy legs," said the lad to the head, and he cast the head up the chimney too.

The third night the lad got into bed, and he heard the bogles striving under the bed, and they had the ball there, and they were casting it to and fro.

Now one of them has his leg thrust out from under the bed, so the lad brings his sword down and cuts it off. Then another thrusts his arm out at other side of the bed, and the lad cuts that off. So at last he had maimed them all, and they all went crying and wailing off, and forgot the ball, but he took it from under the bed, and went to seek his true-love.

Now the lass was taken to York to be hanged; she was brought out on the scaffold, and the hangman said, "Now, lass, thou must hang by the neck till thou be'st dead." But she cried out:

"Stop, stop, I think I see my mother coming!
O mother, hast brought my golden ball
And come to set me free?"

"I've neither brought thy golden ball
Nor come to set thee free,
But I have come to see thee hung
Upon this gallows-tree."

Then the hangman said, "Now, lass, say thy prayers for thou must die." But she said:

"Stop, stop, I think I see my father coming!
O father, hast brought my golden ball
And come to set me free?"

"I've neither brought thy golden ball
Nor come to set thee free,
But I have come to see thee hung
Upon this gallows-tree."

Then the hangman said, "Hast thee done thy prayers? Now, lass, put thy head into the noose."

But she answered, "Stop, stop, I think I see my brother coming!" And again she sang, and then she thought she saw her sister coming, then her uncle, then her aunt, then her cousin; but after this the hangman said, "I will stop no longer, thou 'rt making game of me. Thou must be hung at once."

But now she saw her sweetheart coming through the crowd, and he held over his head in the air her own golden ball; so she said:

"Stop, stop, I see my sweetheart coming!
Sweetheart, hast brought my golden ball
And come to set me free?"

"Aye, I have brought thy golden ball
And come to set thee free,
I have not come to see thee hung
Upon this gallows-tree."

And he took her home, and they lived happy ever after.

My Own Self

In a tiny house in the North Countrie, far away from any town or village, there lived not long ago, a poor widow all alone with her little son, a six-year-old boy.

The house-door opened straight on to the hill-side and all round about were moorlands and huge stones, and swampy hollows; never a house nor a sign of life wherever you might look, for their nearest neighbours were the "ferlies" in the glen below, and the "will-o'-the-wisps" in the long grass along the pathside.

And many a tale she could tell of the "good folk" calling to each other in the oak-trees, and the twinkling lights hopping on to the very window sill, on dark nights; but in spite of the loneliness, she lived on from year to year in the little house, perhaps because she was never asked to pay any rent for it.

But she did not care to sit up late, when the fire burnt low, and no one knew what might be about; so, when they had had their supper she would make up a good fire and go off to bed, so that if anything terrible *did* happen, she could always hide her head under the bed-clothes.

This, however, was far too early to please her little son; so when she called him to bed, he would go on playing beside the fire, as if he did not hear her.

He had always been bad to do with since the day he was born, and his mother did not often care to cross him; indeed, the more she tried to make him obey her, the less heed he paid to anything she said, so it usually ended by his taking his own way.

But one night, just at the fore-end of winter, the widow could not make up her mind to go off to bed, and leave him playing by the fireside; for the wind was tugging at the door, and rattling the window-panes, and well she knew that on such a night, fairies and such like were bound to be out and about, and bent on mischief. So she tried to coax the boy into going at once to bed:

"The safest bed to bide in, such a night as this!" she said: but no, he wouldn't.

Then she threatened to "give him the stick," but it was no use.

The more she begged and scolded, the more he shook his head; and when at last she lost patience and cried that the fairies would surely come and fetch him away, he only laughed and said he wished they *would*, for he would like one to play with.

At that his mother burst into tears, and went off to bed in despair, certain that after such words something dreadful would happen; while her naughty little son sat on his stool by the fire, not at all put out by her crying.

But he had not long been sitting there alone, when he heard a fluttering sound near him in the chimney and presently down by his side dropped the tiniest wee girl you could think of; she was not a span high, and had hair like spun silver, eyes as green as grass, and cheeks red as June roses. The little boy looked at her with surprise.

"Oh!" said he; "what do they call ye?"

"My own self," she said in a shrill but sweet little voice, and she looked at him too. "And what do they call ye?"

"Just my own self too!" he answered cautiously; and with that they began to play together.

She certainly showed him some fine games. She made animals out of the ashes that looked and moved like life; and trees with green leaves waving over tiny houses, with men and women an inch high in them, who, when she breathed on them, fell to walking and talking quite properly.

But the fire was getting low, and the light dim, and presently the little boy stirred the coals with a stick to make them blaze; when out jumped a red-hot cinder, and where should it fall, but on the fairy child's tiny foot.

Thereupon she set up such a squeal, that the boy dropped the stick, and clapped his hands to his ears but it grew to so shrill a screech, that it was like all the wind in the world whistling through one tiny keyhole.

There was a sound in the chimney again, but this time the little boy did not wait to see what it was, but bolted off to bed, where he hid under the blankets and listened in fear and trembling to what went on.

A voice came from the chimney speaking sharply:

"Who's there, and what's wrong?" it said.

"It's my own self," sobbed the fairy-child; "and my foot's burnt sore. O-o-h!"

"Who did it?" said the voice angrily; this time it sounded nearer, and the boy, peeping from under the clothes, could see a white face looking out from the chimney-opening.

"Just my own self too!" said the fairy-child again.

"Then if ye did it your own self," cried the elf-mother shrilly, "what's the use o' making all this fash about it?"—and with that she stretched out a long thin arm, and caught the creature by its ear, and, shaking it roughly, pulled it after her, out of sight up the chimney.

The little boy lay awake a long time, listening, in case the fairy-mother should come back after all; and next evening after supper, his mother was surprised to find that he was willing to go to bed whenever she liked.

"He's taking a turn for the better at last!" she said to herself; but he was thinking just then that, when next a fairy came to play with him, he might not get off quite so easily as he had done this time.

Black Bull of Norroway

In Norroway, long time ago, there lived a certain lady, and she had three daughters: The oldest of them said to her mother: "Mother, bake me a bannock, and roast me a collop, for I'm going away to seek my fortune." Her mother did so; and the daughter went away to an old witch washerwife and told her purpose. The old wife bade her stay that day, and look out of her back-door, and see what she could see. She saw nought the first day. The second day she did the same, and saw nought. On the third day she looked again, and saw a coach-and-six coming along the road. She ran in and told the old wife what she saw. "Well," quoth the old woman, "yon's for you." So they took her into the coach and galloped off.

The second daughter next says to her mother: "Mother, bake me a bannock, and roast me a collop, for I'm going away to seek my fortune." Her mother did so; and away she went to the old wife, as her sister had done. On the third day she looked out of the back-door, and saw a coach-and-four coming along the road. "Well," quoth the old woman, "yon's for you." So they took her in, and off they set.

The third daughter says to her mother: "Mother, bake me a bannock, and roast me a collop, for I'm going away to seek my fortune." Her mother did so; and away she went to the old witch. She bade her look out of her back-door, and see what she could see She did so; and when she came back, said she saw nought. The second day she did the same, and saw nought. The third day she looked again, and on coming back said to the old wife she saw nought but a great Black Bull coming crooning along the road. "Well," quoth the old witch, "yon's for you." On hearing this she was next to distracted with grief and terror; but she was lifted up and set on his back, and away they went.

Aye they travelled, and on they travelled, till the lady grew faint with hunger. "Eat out of my right ear," says the Black Bull, "and drink out of my left ear, and set by your leaving." So she did as he said, and was wonderfully refreshed. And long they rode, and hard they rode, till they came in sight of a very big and bonny castle. "Yonder we must be this night," quoth the Bull; "for my elder brother lives yonder;" and presently they were at the place. They lifted her off his back, and took her in, and sent him away to a park for the night. In the morning, when they brought the Bull home, they took the lady into a fine shining parlour, and gave her a beautiful apple, telling her not to break it till she was in the greatest strait ever mortal was in the world, and that would bring her out of it. Again she was lifted on the Bull's back, and after she had ridden far, and farther than I can tell, they came in sight of a far bonnier castle, and far farther away than the last. Says the Bull to her: "Yonder we must be this night, for my second brother lives yonder;" and they were at the place directly. They lifted her down and took her in, and sent the Bull to the field for the night. In the morning they took the lady into a fine and rich room, and gave her the finest pear she had ever seen, bidding her not to break it till she was in the greatest strait ever mortal could be in, and that would get her out of it. Again she was lifted and set on his back, and away they went. And long they rode, and hard they rode, till they came in sight of the far biggest castle and far farthest off, they had yet seen. "We must be yonder to-night," says the Bull, "for my young brother lives yonder;" and they were there directly. They lifted her down, took her in, and sent the Bull to the field for the night. In the morning they took her into a room, the finest of all, and gave her a plum, telling her not to break it till she was in the greatest strait mortal could be in, and that would get her out of it. Presently they brought home the Bull, set the lady on his back, and away they went.

And aye they rode, and on they rode, till they came to a dark and ugsome glen, where they stopped, and the lady lighted down. Says the Bull to her: "Here you must stay till I go and fight the Old One. You must seat yourself on that stone, and move neither hand nor foot till I come back, else I'll never find you again. And if everything round about you turns blue, I have beaten the Old One; but should all things turn red, he'll have conquered me." She set herself down on the stone, and by-and-by all round her turned blue. Overcome with joy, she lifted one of her feet, and crossed it over the other, so glad was she that her companion was victorious. The Bull returned and sought for her, but never could find her.

Long she sat, and aye she wept, till she wearied. At last she rose and went away, she didn't know where. On she wandered, till she came to a great hill of glass, that she tried all she could to climb, but wasn't able. Round the bottom of the hill she went, sobbing and seeking a passage over, till at last she came to a smith's house; and the smith promised, if she would serve him seven years, he would make her iron shoon, wherewith she could climb over the glassy hill. At seven years' end she got her iron shoon, clomb the glassy hill, and chanced to come to the old washerwife's habitation. There she was told of a gallant young knight that had given in some clothes all over blood to wash, and whoever washed them was to be his wife. The old wife had washed till she was tired, and then she set her daughter at it, and both washed, and they washed, and they washed, in hopes of getting the young knight; but for all they could do they couldn't bring out a stain. At length they set the stranger damsel to work; and whenever she began, the stains came out pure and clean, and the old wife made the knight believe it was her daughter had washed the clothes. So the knight and the eldest daughter were to be married, and the stranger damsel was distracted at the thought of it, for she was deeply in love with him. So she bethought her of her apple and breaking it, found it filled with gold and precious jewellery, the richest she had ever seen. "All these," she said to the eldest daughter, "I will give you, on condition that you put off your marriage for one day and allow me to go into his room alone at night." The lady consented; but meanwhile the old wife had prepared a sleeping drink, and given it to the knight who drank it, and never wakened till next morning. The live-long night the damsel sobbed and sang:

> "Seven long years I served for thee,
> The glassy hill I clomb for thee,
> Thy bloody clothes I wrang for thee;
> And wilt thou not waken and turn to me?"

THE GLASSY HILL I CLOMB FOR THEE

Next day she knew not what to do for grief. Then she broke the pear, and found it filled with jewellery far richer than the contents of the apple. With these jewels she bargained for permission to be a second night in the young knight's chamber; but the old wife gave him another sleeping drink, and again he slept till morning. All night she kept sighing and singing as before:

"Seven long years I served for thee,
The glassy hill I clomb for thee,
Thy bloody clothes I wrang for thee;
And wilt thou not waken and turn to me?"

Still he slept, and she nearly lost hope altogether, But that day, when he was out hunting, somebody asked him what noise and moaning was that they heard all last night in his bedchamber. He said: "I have heard no noise." But they assured him there was; and he resolved to keep waking that night to try what he could hear. That being the third night and the damsel being between hope and despair, she broke her plum, and it held far the richest jewellery of the three. She bargained as before; and the old wife, as before, took in the sleeping drink to the young knight's chamber; but he told her he couldn't drink it that night without sweetening. And when she went away for some honey to sweeten it with, he poured out the drink, and so made the old wife think he had drunk it. They all went to bed again, and the damsel began, as before, singing:

"Seven long years I served for thee,
The glassy hill I clomb for thee,
Thy bloody clothes I wrang for thee;
And wilt thou not waken and turn to me?"

He heard, and turned to her. And she told him all that had befallen her, and he told her all that had happened to him. And he caused the old washerwife and her daughter to be burnt. And they were married, and he and she are living happy to this day for aught I know.

Yallery Brown

Once upon a time, and a very good time it was, though it wasn't in my time, nor in your time, nor any one else's time, there was a young lad of eighteen or so named Tom Tiver working on the Hall Farm. One Sunday he was walking across the west field, 't was a beautiful July night, warm and still and the air was full of little sounds as though the trees and grass were chattering to themselves. And all at once there came a bit ahead of him the pitifullest greetings ever he heard, sob, sobbing, like a bairn spent with fear, and nigh heartbroken; breaking off into a moan and then rising again in a long whimpering wailing that made him feel sick to hark to it. He began to look everywhere for the poor creature. "It must be Sally Bratton's child," he thought to himself; "she was always a flighty thing, and never looked after it. Like as not, she's flaunting about the lanes, and has clean forgot the babby." But though he looked and looked, he could see nought. And presently the whimpering got louder and stronger in the quietness, and he thought he could make out words of some sort. He hearkened with all his ears, and the sorry thing was saying words all mixed up with sobbing—

"Ooh! the stone, the great big stone! ooh! the stones on top!"

Naturally he wondered where the stone might be, and he looked again, and there by the hedge bottom was a great flat stone, nigh buried in the mools, and hid in the cotted grass and weeds. One of the stones was called the "Strangers' Table." However, down he fell on his knee-bones by that stone, and hearkened again. Clearer than ever, but tired and spent with greeting came the little sobbing voice—"Ooh! ooh! the stone, the stone on top." He was gey, and mis-liking to meddle with the thing, but he couldn't stand the whimpering babby, and he tore like mad at the stone, till he felt it lifting from the mools, and all at once it came with a sough out o' the damp earth and the tangled grass and growing things. And there in the hole lay a tiddy thing on its back, blinking up at the moon and at him. 'T was no bigger than a year-old baby, but it had long cotted hair and beard, twisted round and round its body so that you couldn't see its clothes; and the hair was all yaller and shining and silky, like a bairn's; but the face of it was old and as if 't were hundreds of years since 't was young and smooth. Just a heap of wrinkles, and two bright black eyne in the midst, set in a lot of shining yaller hair; and the skin was the colour of the fresh turned earth in the spring—brown as brown could be, and its bare hands and feet were brown like the face of it. The greeting had stopped, but the tears were standing on its cheek, and the tiddy thing looked mazed like in the moonshine and the night air.

The creature's eyne got used like to the moonlight, and presently he looked up in Tom's face as bold as ever was; "Tom," says he, "thou 'rt a good lad!" as cool as thou can think, says he, "Tom, thou 'rt a good lad!" and his voice was soft and high and piping like a little bird twittering.

Tom touched his hat, and began to think what he ought to say. "Houts!" says the thing again, "thou needn't be feared o' me; thou 'st done me a better turn than thou know'st, my lad, and I'll do as much for thee." Tom couldn't speak yet, but he thought; "Lord! for sure 't is a bogle!"

"No!" says he as quick as quick, "I am no bogle, but ye 'd best not ask me what I be; anyways I be a good friend o' thine." Tom's very knee-bones struck, for certainly an ordinary body couldn't have known what he'd been thinking to himself, but he looked so kind like, and spoke so fair, that he made bold to get out, a bit quavery like—

"Might I be axing to know your honour's name?"

"H'm," says he, pulling his beard; "as for that"—and he thought a bit—"ay so," he went on at last, "Yallery Brown thou mayst call me, Yallery Brown; 't is my nature seest thou, and as for a name 't will do as any other. Yallery Brown, Tom, Yallery Brown's thy friend, my lad."

"Thankee, master," says Tom, quite meek like.

"And now," he says, "I'm in a hurry to-night, but tell me quick, what'll I do for thee? Wilt have a wife? I can give thee the finest lass in the town. Wilt be rich? I'll give thee gold as much as thou can carry. Or wilt have help wi' thy work? Only say the word."

Tom scratched his head. "Well, as for a wife, I have no hankering after such; they're but bothersome bodies, and I have women folk at home as 'll mend my clouts; and for gold that's as may be, but for work, there, I can't abide work, and if thou 'lt give me a helpin' hand in it I'll thank—"

"Stop," says he, quick as lightning, "I'll help thee and welcome, but if ever thou sayest that to me—if ever thou thankest me, see'st thou, thou 'lt never see me more. Mind that now; I want no thanks, I'll have no thanks;" and he stampt his tiddy foot on the earth and looked as wicked as a raging bull.

"Mind that now, great lump that thou be," he went on, calming down a bit, "and if ever thou need'st help, or get'st into trouble, call on me and just say, 'Yallery Brown, come from the mools, I want thee!' and I'll be wi' thee at once; and now," says he, picking a dandelion puff, "good-night to thee," and he blowed it up, and it all came into Tom's eyne and ears. Soon as Tom could see again the tiddy creature was gone, and but for the stone on end and the hole at his feet, he'd have thought he'd been dreaming.

Well, Tom went home and to bed; and by the morning he'd nigh forgot all about it. But when he went to the work, there was none to do! all was done already, the horses seen to, the stables cleaned out, everything in its proper place, and he'd nothing to do but sit with his hands in his pockets. And so it went on day after day, all the work done by Yallery Brown, and better done, too, than he could have done it himself. And if the master gave him more work, he sat down, and the work did itself, the singeing irons, or the broom, or what not, set to, and with ne'er a hand put to it would get through in no time. For he never saw Yallery Brown in daylight; only in the darklins he saw him hopping about, like a Will-o-th'-wyke without his lanthorn.

At first 't was mighty fine for Tom; he'd nought to do and good pay for it; but by-and-by things began to grow vicey-varsy. If the work was done for Tom, 't was undone for the other lads; if his buckets were filled, theirs were upset; if his tools were sharpened, theirs were blunted and spoiled; if his horses were clean as daisies, theirs were splashed with muck, and so on; day in and day out, 't was the same. And the lads saw Yallery Brown flitting about o' nights, and they saw the things working without hands o' days, and they saw that Tom's work was done for him, and theirs undone for them; and naturally they begun to look shy on him, and they wouldn't speak or come nigh him, and they carried tales to the master and so things went from bad to worse.

For Tom could do nothing himself; the brooms wouldn't stay in his hand, the plough ran away from him, the hoe kept out of his grip. He thought that he'd do his own work after all, so that Yallery Brown would leave him and his neighbours alone. But he couldn't—true as death he couldn't. He could only sit by and look on, and have the cold shoulder turned on him, while the unnatural thing was meddling with the others, and working for him.

At last, things got so bad that the master gave Tom the sack, and if he hadn't, all the rest of the lads would have sacked him, for they swore they'd not stay on the same garth with Tom. Well, naturally Tom felt bad; 't was a very good place, and good pay too; and he was fair mad with Yallery Brown, as 'd got him into such a trouble. So Tom shook his fist in the air and called out as loud as he could, "Yallery Brown, come from the mools; thou scamp, I want thee!"

You'll scarce believe it, but he'd hardly brought out the words but he felt something tweaking his leg behind, while he jumped with the smart of it; and soon as he looked down, there was the tiddy thing, with his shining hair, and wrinkled face, and wicked glinting black eyne.

Tom was in a fine rage, and he would have liked to have kicked him, but 't was no good, there wasn't enough of it to get his boot against; but he said, "Look here, master, I'll thank thee to leave me alone after this, dost hear? I want none of thy help, and I'll have nought more to do with thee—see now."

The horrid thing broke into a screeching laugh, and pointed its brown finger at Tom. "Ho, ho, Tom!" says he. "Thou 'st thanked me, my lad, and I told thee not, I told thee not!"

"I don't want thy help, I tell thee," Tom yelled at him—"I only want never to see thee again, and to have nought more to do with 'ee—thou can go."

The thing only laughed and screeched and mocked, as long as Tom went on swearing, but so soon as his breath gave out—

"Tom, my lad," he said with a grin, "I'll tell 'ee summat, Tom. True's true I'll never help thee again, and call as thou wilt, thou 'lt never see me after to-day; but I never said that I'd leave thee alone, Tom, and I never will, my lad! I was nice and safe under the stone, Tom, and could do no harm; but thou let me out thyself, and thou can't put me back again! I would have been thy friend and worked for thee if thou had been wise; but since thou bee'st no more than a born fool I'll give 'ee no more than a born fool's luck; and when all goes vicey-varsy, and everything agee—thou 'lt mind that it's Yallery Brown's doing though m'appen thou doesn't see him. Mark my words, will 'ee?"

And he began to sing, dancing round Tom, like a bairn with his yellow hair, but looking older than ever with his grinning wrinkled bit of a face:

"Work as thou will
Thou 'lt never do well;
Work as thou mayst
Thou 'lt never gain grist;
For harm and mischance and Yallery Brown
Thou 'st let out thyself from under the stone."

Tom could never rightly mind what he said next. 'T was all cussing and calling down misfortune on him; but he was so mazed in fright that he could only stand there shaking all over, and staring down at the horrid thing; and if he'd gone on long, Tom would have tumbled down in a fit. But by-and-by, his yaller shining hair rose up in the air, and wrapt itself round him till he looked for all the world like a great dandelion puff; and it floated away on the wind over the wall and out o' sight, with a parting skirl of wicked voice and sneering laugh.

And did it come true, sayst thou? My word! but it did, sure as death! He worked here and he worked there, and turned his hand to this and to that, but it always went agee, and 't was all Yallery Brown's doing. And the children died, and the crops rotted—the beasts never fatted, and nothing ever did well with him; and till he was dead and buried, and m'appen even afterwards, there was no end to Yallery Brown's spite at him; day in and day out he used to hear him saying—

"Work as thou wilt
Thou 'lt never do well;
Work as thou mayst
Thou 'lt never gain grist;
For harm and mischance and Yallery Brown
Thou 'st let out thyself from under the stone."

Three Feathers

Once upon a time there was a girl who was married to a husband that she never saw. And the way this was, was that he was only at home at night, and would never have any light in the house. The girl thought that was funny, and all her friends told her there must be something wrong with her husband, some great deformity that made him want not to be seen.

Well, one night when he came home she suddenly lit a candle and saw him. He was handsome enough to make all the women of the world fall in love with him. But scarcely had she seen him when he began to change into a bird, and then he said: "Now you have seen me, you shall see me no more, unless you are willing to serve seven years and a day for me, so that I may become a man once more." Then he told her to take three feathers from under his side, and whatever she wished through them would come to pass. Then he left her at a great house to be laundry-maid for seven years and a day.

And the girl used to take the feathers and say:

"By virtue of my three feathers may the copper be lit, and the clothes washed, and mangled, and folded, and put away to the missus's satisfaction."

And then she had no more care about it. The feathers did the rest, and the lady set great store by her for a better laundress she had never had. Well, one day the butler, who had a notion to have the pretty laundry-maid for his wife, said to her, he should have spoken before but he did not want to vex her. "Why should it when I am but a fellow-servant?" the girl said. And then he felt free to go on, and explain he had £70 laid by with the master, and how would she like him for a husband.

And the girl told him to fetch her the money, and he asked his master for it, and brought it to her. But as they were going up-stairs, she cried, "O John, I must go back, sure I've left my shutters undone, and they'll be slashing and banging all night."

The butler said, "Never you trouble, I'll put them right." and he ran back, while she took her feathers, and said: "By virtue of my three feathers may the shutters slash and bang till morning, and John not be able to fasten them nor yet to get his fingers free from them."

And so it was. Try as he might the butler could not leave hold, nor yet keep the shutters from blowing open as he closed them. And he *was* angry, but could not help himself, and he did not care to tell of it and get the laugh on him, so no one knew.

Then after a bit the coachman began to notice her, and she found he had some £40 with the master, and he said she might have it if she would take him with it.

So after the laundry-maid had his money in her apron as they went merrily along, she stopt, exclaiming: "My clothes are left outside, I must run back and bring them in." "Stop for me while I go; it is a cold frost night," said William, "you'd be catching your death." So the girl waited long enough to take her feathers out and say, "By virtue of my three feathers may the clothes slash and blow about till morning, and may William not be able to take his hand from them nor yet to gather them up." And then she was away to bed and to sleep.

The coachman did not want to be every one's jest, and he said nothing. So after a bit the footman comes to her and said he: "I have been with my master for years and have saved up a good bit, and you have been three years here, and must have saved up as well. Let us put it together, and make us a home or else stay on at service as pleases you." Well, she got him to bring the savings to her as the others had, and then she pretended she was faint, and said to him: "James, I feel so queer, run down cellar for me, that's a dear, and fetch me up a drop of brandy." Now no sooner had he started than she said: "By virtue of my three feathers may there be slashing and spilling, and James not be able to pour the brandy straight nor yet to take his hand from it until morning."

And so it was. Try as he might James could not get his glass filled, and there was slashing and spilling, and right on it all, down came the master to know what it meant!

So James told him he could not make it out, but he could not get the drop of brandy the laundry-maid had asked for, and his hand would shake and spill everything, and yet come away he could not.

This got him in for a regular scrape, and the master when he got back to his wife said: "What has come over the men, they were all right until that laundry-maid of yours came. Something is up now though. They have all drawn out their pay, and yet they don't leave, and what can it be anyway?"

But his wife said she could not hear of the laundry-maid being blamed, for she was the best servant she had and worth all the rest put together.

So it went on until one day as the girl stood in the hall door, the coachman happened to say to the footman: "Do you know how that girl served me, James?" And then William told about the clothes. The butler put in, "That was nothing to what she served me," and he told of the shutters clapping all night.

Just then the master came through the hall, and the girl said: "By virtue of my three feathers may there be slashing and striving between master and men, and may all get splashed in the pond."

And so it was, the men fell to disputing which had suffered the most by her, and when the master came up all would be heard at once and none listened to him, and it came to blows all round, and the first they knew they had shoved one another into the pond.

When the girl thought they had had enough she took the spell off, and the master asked her what had begun the row, for he had not heard in the confusion.

And the girl said: "They were ready to fall on any one; they'd have beat me if you had not come by."

So it blew over for that time, and through her feathers she made the best laundress ever known. But to make a long story short, when the seven years and a day were up, the bird-husband, who had known her doings all along, came after her, restored to his own shape again. And he told her mistress he had come to take her from being a servant, and that she should have servants under her. But he did not tell of the feathers.

And then he bade her give the men back their savings.

"That was a rare game you had with them," said he, "but now you are going where there is plenty, leave them each their own." So she did; and they drove off to their castle, where they lived happy ever after.

Sir Gammer Vans

Last Sunday morning at six o'clock in the evening as I was sailing over the tops of the mountains in my little boat, I met two men on horseback riding on one mare: So I asked them, "Could they tell me whether the little old woman was dead yet who was hanged last Saturday week for drowning herself in a shower of feathers?" They said they could not positively inform me, but if I went to Sir Gammer Vans he could tell me all about it. "But how am I to know the house?" said I. "Ho, 't is easy enough," said they, "for 't is a brick house, built entirely of flints, standing alone by itself in the middle of sixty or seventy others just like it."

"Oh, nothing in the world is easier," said I.

"Nothing *can* be easier," said they: so I went on my way.

Now this Sir G. Vans was a giant, and a bottle-maker. And as all giants who *are* bottle-makers usually pop out of a little thumb-bottle from behind the door, so did Sir G. Vans.

"How d'ye do?" says he.

"Very well, I thank you," says I.

"Have some breakfast with me?"

"With all my heart," says I.

So he gave me a slice of beer, and a cup of cold veal; and there was a little dog under the table that picked up all the crumbs.

"Hang him," says I.

"No, don't hang him," says he; "for he killed a hare yesterday. And if you don't believe me, I'll show you the hare alive in a basket."

So he took me into his garden to show me the curiosities. In one corner there was a fox hatching eagle's eggs; in another there was an iron apple tree, entirely covered with pears and lead; in the third there was the hare which the dog killed yesterday alive in the basket; and in the fourth there were twenty-four *hipper switches* threshing tobacco, and at the sight of me they threshed so hard that they drove the plug through the wall, and through a little dog that was passing by on the other side. I, hearing the dog howl, jumped over the wall; and turned it as neatly inside out as possible, when it ran away as if it had not an hour to live. Then he took me into the park to show me his deer: and I remembered that I had a warrant in my pocket to shoot venison for his majesty's dinner. So I set fire to my bow, poised my arrow, and shot amongst them. I broke seventeen ribs on one side, and twenty-one and a half on the other; but my arrow passed clean through without ever touching it, and the worst was I lost my arrow: however, I found it again in the hollow of a tree. I felt it; it felt clammy. I smelt it; it smelt honey. "Oh, ho," said I, "here's a bee's nest," when out sprang a covey of partridges. I shot at them; some say I killed eighteen; but I am sure I killed thirty-six, besides a dead salmon which was flying over the bridge, of which I made the best apple-pie I ever tasted.

Tom Hickathrift

Before the days of William the Conqueror there dwelt a man in the marsh of the Isle of Ely whose name was Thomas Hickathrift, a poor day labourer, but so stout that he could do two days' work in one. His one son he called by his own name, Thomas Hickathrift, and he put him to good learning, but the lad was none of the wisest, and indeed seemed to be somewhat soft, so he got no good at all from his teaching.

Tom's father died, and his mother being tender of him, kept him as well as she could. The slothful fellow would do nothing but sit in the chimney-corner, and eat as much at a time as would serve four or five ordinary men. And so much did he grow that when but ten years old he was already eight feet high, and his hand like a shoulder of mutton.

One day his mother went to a rich farmer's house to beg a bottle of straw for herself and Tom. "Take what you will," said the farmer, an honest charitable man. So when she got home she told Tom to fetch the straw, but he wouldn't and, beg as she might, he wouldn't till she borrowed him a cart rope. So off he went, and when he came to the farmer's, master and men were all a-trashing in the barn.

"I'm come for the straw," said Tom.

"Take as much as thou canst carry," said the farmer.

So Tom laid down his rope and began to make his bottle.

"Your rope is too short," said the farmer by way of a joke; but the joke was on Tom's side, for when he had made up his load there was some twenty hundred-weight of straw, and though they called him a fool for thinking he could carry the tithe of it, he flung it over his shoulder as if it had been a hundred-weight, to the great admiration of master and men.

Tom's strength being thus made known there was no longer any basking by the fire for him; every one would be hiring him to work, and telling him 't was a shame to live such a lazy life. So Tom seeing them wait on him as they did, went to work first with one, then with another. And one day a woodman desired his help to bring home a tree. Off went Tom and four men besides, and when they came to the tree they began to draw it into the cart with pulleys. At last Tom, seeing them unable to lift it, "Stand away, you fools," said he, and taking the tree, set it on one end and laid it in the cart. "Now," said he, "see what a man can do." "Marry, 't is true," said they, and the woodman asked what reward he'd take. "Oh, a stick for my mother's fire," said Tom; and espying a tree bigger than was in the cart, he laid it on his shoulders and went home with it as fast as the cart and six horses could draw it.

Tom now saw that he had more strength than twenty men, and began to be very merry, taking delight in company, in going to fairs and meetings, in seeing sports and pastimes. And at cudgels, wrestling, or throwing the hammer, not a man could stand against him, so that at last none durst go into the ring to wrestle with him, and his fame was spread more and more in the country.

Far and near he would go to any meetings, as football play or the like. And one day in a part of the country where he was a stranger, and none knew him, he stopped to watch the company at football play; rare sport it was; but Tom spoiled it all, for meeting the ball he took it such a kick that away it flew none could tell whither. They were angry with Tom as you may fancy, but got nothing by that as Tom took hold of a big spar, and laid about with a will, so that though the whole country-side was up in arms against him, he cleared his way wherever he came.

It was late in the evening ere he could turn homeward, and on the road there met him four lusty rogues that had been robbing passengers all day. They thought they had a good prize in Tom, who was all alone, and made cocksure of his money.

"Stand and deliver!" said they.

"What should I deliver?" said Tom.

"Your money, sirrah," said they.

"You shall give me better words for it first," said Tom.

"Come, come, no more prating; money we want, and money we'll have before you stir."

"Is it so?" said Tom, "nay, then come and take it."

The long and the short of it was that Tom killed two of the rogues and grievously wounded the other two, and took all their money, which was as much as two hundred pounds. And when he came home he made his old mother laugh with the story of how he served the football players and the four thieves.

But you shall see that Tom sometimes met his match. In wandering one day in the forest he met a lusty tinker that had a good staff on his shoulder, and a great dog to carry his bag and tools.

"Whence come you and whither are you going?" said Tom, "this is no highway."

"What's that to you?" said the tinker; "fools must needs be meddling."

"I'll make you know," said Tom, "before you and I part, what it is to me."

"Well," said the tinker, "I'm ready for a bout with any man, and I hear there is one Tom Hickathrift in the country of whom great things are told. I'd fain see him to have a turn with him."

"Ay," said Tom, "methinks he might be master with you. Anyhow, I am the man; what have you to say to me?"

"Why, verily, I'm glad we are so happily met."

"Sure, you do but jest," said Tom.

"Marry, I'm in earnest," said the tinker. "A match?" "'T is done." "Let me first get a twig," said Tom. "Ay," said the tinker, "hang him that would fight a man unarmed."

So Tom took a gate-rail for his staff, and at it they fell, the tinker at Tom, and Tom at the tinker, like two giants they laid on at each other. The tinker had a leathern coat on, and at every blow Tom gave the tinker his coat roared again, yet the tinker did not give way one inch. At last Tom gave him a blow on the side of his head which felled him.

"Now tinker where are you?" said Tom.

But the tinker being a nimble fellow, leapt up again, gave Tom a blow that made him reel again, and followed his blow with one on the other side that made Tom's neck crack again. So Tom flung down his weapon and yielded the tinker the better on it, took him home to his house, where they nursed their bruises and from that day forth there was no stauncher pair of friends than they two.

Tom's fame was thus spread abroad till at length a brewer at Lynn, wanting a good lusty man to carry his beer to Wisbeach went to hire Tom, and promised him a new suit of clothes from top to toe, and that he should eat and drink of the best, so Tom yielded to be his man and his master told him what way he should go, for you must understand there was a monstrous giant who kept part of the marsh-land, so that none durst go that way.

So Tom went every day to Wisbeach a good twenty miles by the road. 'T was a wearisome journey thought Tom and he soon found that the way kept by the giant was nearer by half. Now Tom had got more strength than ever, being well kept as he was and drinking so much strong ale as he did. One day, then, as he was going to Wisbeach, without saying anything to his master or any of his fellow servants, he resolved to take the nearest road or to lose his life; as they say, to win horse or lose saddle. Thus resolved, he took the near road, flinging open the gates for his cart and horses to go through. At last the giant spied him, and came up speedily, intending to take his beer for a prize.

He met Tom like a lion as though he would have swallowed him. "Who gave you authority to come this way?" roared he. "I'll make you an example for all rogues under the sun. See how many heads hang on yonder tree. Yours shall hang higher than all the rest for a warning."

But Tom made him answer, "A fig in your teeth you shall not find me like one of them, traitorly rogue that you are."

The giant took these words in high disdain, and ran into his cave to fetch his great club, intending to dash out Tom's brains at the first blow.

Tom knew not what to do for a weapon; his whip would be but little good against a monstrous beast twelve foot in length and six foot about the waist. But whilst the giant went for his club, bethinking him of a very good weapon, he made no more ado, but took his cart, turned it upside down, and took axle-tree and wheel for shield and buckler. And very good weapons they were found!

Out came the giant and began to stare at Tom. "You are like to do great service with those weapons," roared he. "I have here a twig that will beat you and your wheel to the ground." Now this twig was as thick as some mileposts are, but Tom was not daunted for all that, though the giant made at him with such force that the wheel cracked again. But Tom gave as good as he got, taking the giant such a weighty blow on the side of the head that he reeled again. "What," said Tom, "are you drunk with my strong beer already?"

So at it they went, Tom laying such huge blows at the giant, down whose face sweat and blood ran together, so that, being fat and foggy and tired with the long fighting, he asked Tom would he let him drink a little? "Nay, nay," said Tom, "my mother did not teach me such wit; who'd be a fool then?" And seeing the giant beginning to weary and fail in his blows, Tom thought best to make hay whilst the sun shone, and, laying on as fast as though he had been mad, he brought the giant to the ground. In vain were the giant's roars and prayers and promises to yield himself and be Tom's servant. Tom laid at him till he was dead, and then, cutting off his head, he went into the cave, and found a great store of silver and gold, which made his heart to leap. So he loaded his cart, and after delivering his beer at Wisbeach, he came home and told his master what had befallen him. And on the morrow he and his master and more of the towns-folk of Lynn set out for the giant's cave. Tom showed them the head, and what silver and gold there was in the cave, and not a man but leapt for joy, for the giant was a great enemy to all the country.

The news was spread all up and down the country-side how Tom Hickathrift had killed the giant. And well was he that could run to see the cave; all the folk made bonfires for joy, and if Tom was respected before, he was much more so now. With common consent he took possession of the cave and every one said, had it been twice as much, he would have deserved it. So Tom pulled down the cave, and built himself a brave house. The ground that the giant kept by force for himself, Tom gave part to the poor for their common land, and part he turned into good wheat-land to keep himself and his old mother, Jane Hickathrift. And now he was become the chiefest man in the country-side; 't was no longer plain Tom, but Mr. Hickathrift, and he was held in due respect I promise you. He kept men and maids and lived most bravely; made him a park to keep deer, and time passed with him happily in his great house till the end of his days.

The Hedley Kow

There was once an old woman, who earned a poor living by going errands and such like, for the farmers' wives round about the village where she lived. It wasn't much she earned by it; but with a plate of meat at one house, and a cup of tea at another, she made shift to get on somehow, and always looked as cheerful as if she hadn't a want in the world.

Well, one summer evening as she was trotting away homewards, she came upon a big black pot lying at the side of the road.

"Now *that*," said she, stopping to look at it, "would be just the very thing for me if I had anything to put into it! But who can have left it here?" and she looked round about, as if the person it belonged to must be not far off. But she could see no one.

"Maybe it'll have a hole in it," she said thoughtfully:—

"Ay, that'll be how they've left it lying, hinny. But then it 'd do fine to put a flower in for the window; I'm thinking I'll just take it home, anyways." And she bent her stiff old back, and lifted the lid to look inside.

"Mercy me!" she cried, and jumped back to the other side of the road; "*if it is fit brim full o' gold* PIECES!!"

For a while she could do nothing but walk round and round her treasure, admiring the yellow gold and wondering at her good luck, and saying to herself about every two minutes, "Well, I *do* be feeling rich and grand!" But presently she began to think how she could best take it home with her; and she couldn't see any other way than by fastening one end of her shawl to it, and so dragging it after her along the road.

"It'll certainly be soon dark," she said to herself, "and folk'll not see what I'm bringing home with me, and so I'll have all the night to myself to think what I'll do with it. I could buy a grand house and all, and live like the Queen herself, and not do a stroke of work all day, but just sit by the fire with a cup of tea; or maybe I'll give it to the priest to keep for me, and get a piece as I'm wanting; or maybe I'll just bury it in a hole at the garden-foot, and put a bit on the chimney, between the chiney teapot and the spoons—for ornament like. Ah! I feel so grand, I don't know myself rightly!"

And by this time, being already rather tired with dragging such a heavy weight after her, she stopped to rest for a minute, turning to make sure that her treasure was safe.

But when she looked at it, it wasn't a pot of gold at all, but a great lump of shining silver!

She stared at it, and rubbed her eyes and stared at it again; but she couldn't make it look like anything but a great lump of silver. "I'd have sworn it was a pot of gold," she said at last, "but I reckon I must have been dreaming. Ay, now, that's a change for the better; it'll be far less trouble to look after, and none so easy stolen; yon gold pieces would have been a sight of bother to keep 'em safe. Ay, I'm well quit of them; and with my bonny lump I'm as rich as rich—!"

And she set off homewards again, cheerfully planning all the grand things she was going to do with her money. It wasn't very long, however, before she got tired again and stopped once more to rest for a minute or two.

Again she turned to look at her treasure, and as soon as she set eyes on it she cried out in astonishment. "Oh, my!" said she; "now it's a lump o' iron! Well, that beats all; and it's just real convenient! I can sell it as *easy* as *easy*, and get a lot o' penny pieces for it. Ay, hinny, an' it's much handier than a lot o' yer gold and silver as 'd have kept me from sleeping o' nights thinking the neighbours were robbing me—an' it's a real good thing to have by you in a house, ye niver can tell what ye mightn't use it for, an' it'll sell—ay, for a real lot. Rich? I'll be just *rolling!*"

And on she trotted again chuckling to herself on her good luck, till presently she glanced over her shoulder, "just to make sure it was there still," as she said to herself.

"Eh, my!" she cried as soon as she saw it; "if it hasn't gone and turned itself into a great stone this time! Now, how could it have known that I was just *terrible* wanting something to hold my door open with? Ay, if that isn't a good change! Hinny, it's a fine thing to have such good luck."

And, all in a hurry to see how the stone would look in its corner by her door, she trotted off down the hill, and stopped at the foot, beside her own little gate.

When she had unlatched it, she turned to unfasten her shawl from the stone, which this time seemed to lie unchanged and peaceably on the path beside her, There was still plenty of light, and she could see the stone quite plainly as she bent her stiff back over it, to untie the shawl end; when, all of a sudden, it seemed to give a jump and a squeal, and grew in a moment as big as a great horse; then it threw down four lanky legs, and shook out two long ears, flourished a tail, and went off kicking its feet into the and laughing like a naughty mocking boy.

The old woman stared after it, till it was fairly out of sight.

"WELL!" she said at last, "I *do* be the luckiest body hereabouts! Fancy me seeing the Hedley Kow all to myself, and making so free with it too! I can tell you, I *do* feel that GRAND—"

And she went into her cottage, and sat down by the fire to think over her good luck.

Gobborn Seer

Once there was a man Gobborn Seer, and he had a son called Jack.

One day he sent him out to sell a sheep skin, and Gobborn said, "You must bring me back the skin and the value of it as well."

So Jack started, but he could not find any who would leave him the skin and give him its price too. So he came home discouraged.

But Gobborn Seer said, "Never mind, you must take another turn at it to-morrow."

So he tried again, and nobody wished to buy the skin on those terms.

When he came home his father said, "You must go and try your luck to-morrow," and the third day it seemed as if it would be the same thing over again. And he had half a mind not to go back at all, his father would be so vexed. As he came to a bridge, like the Creek Road one yonder, he leaned on the parapet thinking of his trouble, and that perhaps it would be foolish to run away from home, but he could not tell which to do; when he saw a girl washing her clothes on the bank below. She looked up and said:

"If it may be no offence asking, what is it you feel so badly about?"

"My father has given me this skin, and I am to fetch it back and the price of it beside."

"Is that all? Give it here, and it's easy done."

So the girl washed the skin in the stream, took the wool from it, and paid him the value of it, and gave him the skin to carry back.

His father was well pleased, and said to Jack, "That was a witty woman; she would make you a good wife. Do you think you could tell her again?"

Jack thought he could, so his father told him to go by-and-by to the bridge, and see if she was there, and if so bid her come home to take tea with them.

And sure enough Jack spied her and told her how his old father had a wish to meet her, and would she be pleased to drink tea with them.

The girl thanked him kindly, and said she could come the next day; she was too busy at the moment.

"All the better," said Jack, "I'll have time to make ready."

So when she came Gobborn Seer could see she was a witty woman, and he asked her if she would marry his Jack. She said "Yes," and they were married.

Not long after, Jack's father told him he must come with him and build the finest castle that ever was seen, for a king who wished to outdo all others by his wonderful castle.

And as they went to lay the foundation-stone, Gobborn Seer said to Jack, "Can't you shorten the way for me?"

But Jack looked ahead and there was a long road before them, and he said, "I don't see, father, how I could break a bit off."

"You're no good to me, then, and had best be off home."

So poor Jack turned back, and when he came in his wife said, "Why, how's this you've come alone?" and he told her what his father had said and his answer.

"You stupid," said his witty wife, "if you had told a tale you would have shortened the road! Now listen till I tell you a story, and then catch up with Gobborn Seer and begin it at once. He will like hearing it, and by the time you are done you will have reached the foundation-stone."

So Jack sweated and overtook his father. Gobborn Seer said never a word, but Jack began his story, and the road was shortened as his wife had said.

When they came to the end of their journey, they started building of this castle which was to outshine all others. Now the wife had advised them to be intimate with the servants, and so they did as she said, and it was "Good-morning" and "Good-day to you" as they passed in and out.

Now, at the end of a twelvemonth, Gobborn, the wise man, had built such a castle thousands were gathered to admire it.

And the king said: "The castle is done. I shall return to-morrow and pay you all."

"I have just a ceiling to finish in an upper lobby," said Gobborn, "and then it wants nothing."

But after the king was gone off, the housekeeper sent for Gobborn and Jack, and told them that she had watched for a chance to warn them, for the king was so afraid they should carry their art away and build some other king as fine a castle, he meant to take their lives on the morrow. Gobborn told Jack to keep a good heart, and they would come off all right.

When the king had come back Gobborn told him he had been unable to complete the job for lack of a tool left at home, and he should like to send Jack after it.

"No, no," said the king, "cannot one of the men do the errand?"

"No, they could not make themselves understood," said the Seer, "but Jack could do the errand."

"You and your son are to stop here. But how will it do if I send my own son?"

"That will do."

So Gobborn sent by him a message to Jack's wife. "Give him *Crooked and Straight*!"

Now there was a little hole in the wall rather high up, and Jack's wife tried to reach up into a chest there after "crooked and straight," but at last she asked the king's son to help her, because his arms were longest.

But when he was leaning over the chest she caught him by the two heels, and threw him into the chest, and fastened it down. So there he was, both "crooked and straight!"

Then he begged for pen and ink, which she brought him, but he was not allowed out, and holes were bored that he might breathe.

When his letter came, telling the king, his father, he was to be let free when Gobborn and Jack were safe home, the king saw he must settle for the building, and let them come away.

As they left Gobborn told him: Now that Jack was done with this work, he should soon build a castle for his witty wife far superior to the king's, which he did, and they lived there happily ever after.

Lawkamercyme

There was an old woman, as I've heard tell.
She went to the market her eggs for to sell;
She went to the market, all on a market-day,
And she fell asleep on the king's highway.

There came by a pedlar, whose name was Stout,
He cut her petticoats round about;
He cut her petticoats up to the knees,
Which made the old woman to shiver and freeze.

When this old woman first did wake,
She began to shiver, and she began to shake;
She began to wonder, and she began to cry—
"Lawkamercyme, this is none of I!"

"But if it be I, as I do hope it be,
I've a little dog at home, and he'll know me;
If it be I, he'll wag his little tail,
And if it be not I, he'll loudly bark and wail."

Home went the little woman, all in the dark;
Up got the little dog, and he began to bark;
He began to bark, so she began to cry—
"Lawkamercyme, this is none of I!"

Tattercoats

In a great Palace by the sea there once dwelt a very rich old lord, who had neither wife nor children living, only one little granddaughter, whose face he had never seen in all her life. He hated her bitterly, because at her birth his favourite daughter died; and when the old nurse brought him the baby, he swore, that it might live or die as it liked, but he would never look on its face as long as it lived.

So he turned his back, and sat by his window looking out over the sea, and weeping great tears for his lost daughter, till his white hair and beard grew down over his shoulders and twined round his chair and crept into the chinks of the floor, and his tears, dropping on to the window-ledge, wore a channel through the stone, and ran away in a little river to the great sea. And, meanwhile, his granddaughter grew up with no one to care for her, or clothe her; only the old nurse, when no one was by, would sometimes give her a dish of scraps from the kitchen, or a torn petticoat from the rag-bag; while the other servants of the Palace would drive her from the house with blows and mocking words, calling her "Tattercoats," and pointing at her bare feet and shoulders, till she ran away crying, to hide among the bushes.

And so she grew up, with little to eat or wear, spending her days in the fields and lanes, with only the gooseherd for a companion, who would play to her so merrily on his little pipe, when she was hungry, or cold, or tired, that she forgot all her troubles, and fell to dancing, with his flock of noisy geese for partners.

But, one day, people told each other that the King was travelling through the land, and in the town near by was to give a great ball, to all the lords and ladies of the country, when the Prince, his only son, was to choose a wife.

One of the royal invitations was brought to the Palace by the sea, and the servants carried it up to the old lord who still sat by his window, wrapped in his long white hair and weeping into the little river that was fed by his tears.

But when he heard the King's command, he dried his eyes and bade them bring shears to cut him loose, for his hair had bound him a fast prisoner and he could not move. And then he sent them for rich clothes, and jewels, which he put on; and he ordered them to saddle the white horse, with gold and silk, that he might ride to meet the King.

Meanwhile Tattercoats had heard of the great doings in the town, and she sat by the kitchen-door weeping because she could not go to see them. And when the old nurse heard her crying she went to the Lord of the Palace, and begged him to take his granddaughter with him to the King's ball.

But he only frowned and told her to be silent, while the servants laughed and said: "Tattercoats is happy in her rags, playing with the gooseherd, let her be—it is all she is fit for."

A second, and then a third time, the old nurse begged him to let the girl go with him, but she was answered only by black looks and fierce words, till she was driven from the room by the jeering servants, with blows and mocking words.

Weeping over her ill-success, the old nurse went to look for Tattercoats; but the girl had been turned from the door by the cook, and had run away to tell her friend the gooseherd, how unhappy she was because she could not go to the King's ball.

But when the gooseherd had listened to her story, he bade her cheer up, and proposed that they should go together into the town to see the King, and all the fine things; and when she looked sorrowfully down at her rags and bare feet, he played a note or two upon his pipe, so gay and merry, that she forgot all about her tears and her troubles, and before she well knew, the herdboy had taken her by the hand, and she, and he, and the geese before them, were dancing down the road towards the town.

Before they had gone very far, a handsome young man, splendidly dressed, rode up and stopped to ask the way to the castle where the King was staying; and when he found that they too were going thither, he got off his horse and walked beside them along the road.

The herdboy pulled out his pipe and played a low sweet tune, and the stranger looked again and again at Tattercoats' lovely face till he fell deeply in love with her, and begged her to marry him.

But she only laughed, and shook her golden head.

"You would be finely put to shame if you had a goosegirl for your wife!" said she; "go and ask one of the great ladies you will see to-night at the King's ball, and do not flout poor Tattercoats."

But the more she refused him the sweeter the pipe played, and the deeper the young man fell in love; till at last he begged her, as a proof of his sincerity, to come that night at twelve to the King's ball, just as she was, with the herdboy and his geese, and in her torn petticoat and bare feet, and he would dance with her before the King and the lords and ladies, and present her to them all, as his dear and honoured bride.

So when night came, and the hall in the castle was full of light and music, and the lords and ladies were dancing before the King, just as the clock struck twelve, Tattercoats and the herdboy, followed by his flock of noisy geese, entered at the great doors, and walked straight up the ball-room, while on either side the ladies whispered, the lords laughed, and the King seated at the far end stared in amazement.

But as they came in front of the throne, Tattercoats' lover rose from beside the King, and came to meet her. Taking her by the hand, he kissed her thrice before them all, and turned to the King.

TATTERCOATS.

"Father!" he said, for it was the Prince himself, "I have made my choice, and here is my bride, the loveliest girl in all the land, and the sweetest as well!"

Before he had finished speaking, the herdboy put his pipe to his lips and played a few low notes that sounded like a bird singing far off in the woods; and as he played, Tattercoats' rags were changed to shining robes sewn with glittering jewels, a golden crown lay upon her golden hair, and the flock of geese behind her, became a crowd of dainty pages, bearing her long train.

And as the King rose to greet her as his daughter, the trumpets sounded loudly in honour of the new Princess, and the people outside in the street said to each other:

"Ah! now the Prince has chosen for his wife the loveliest girl in all the land!"

But the gooseherd was never seen again, and no one knew what became of him; while the old lord went home once more to his Palace by the sea, for he could not stay at Court, when he had sworn never to look on his granddaughter's face.

So there he still sits by his window, if you could only see him, as you some day may, weeping more bitterly than ever, as he looks out over the sea.

The Wee Bannock

"Grannie, grannie, come tell us the story of the wee bannock."

"Hout, childer, ye've heard it a hundred times afore. I needn't tell it over again."

"Ah! but, grannie, it's such a fine one. You must tell it. Just once."

"Well, well, if ye'll all promise to be good, I'll tell it ye again."

There lived an old man and an old woman at the side of a burn. They had two cows, five hens, and a cock, a cat and two kittens. The old man looked after the cows, and the old wife span on the distaff. The kittens oft gripped at the old wife's spindle, as it tussled over the hearthstone. "Sho, sho," she would say, "go away;" and so it tussled about.

One day, after breakfast, she thought she would have a bannock. So she baked two oatmeal bannocks, and set them on to the fire to harden. After a while, the old man came in, and sat down beside the fire, and takes one of the bannocks, and snaps it through the middle. When the other one sees this, it runs off as fast as it could, and the old wife after it, with the spindle in the one hand, and the distaff in the other. But the wee bannock ran away and out of sight, and ran till it came to a pretty large thatched house, and it ran boldly up inside to the fireside; and there were three tailors sitting on a big bench. When they saw the wee bannock come in, they jumped up, and got behind the goodwife, that was carding tow by the fire. "Hout," quoth she, "be no afeard; it's but a wee bannock. Grip it, and I'll give ye a sup of milk with it." Up she gets with the tow-cards and the tailor with the goose, and the two 'prentices, the one with the big shears, and the other with the lawbrod; but it dodged them, and ran round about the fire; and one of the 'prentices, thinking to snap it with the shears, fell into the ashes. The tailor cast the goose, and the goodwife the tow-cards; but it wouldn't do. The bannock ran away, and ran till it came to a wee house at the roadside; and in it runs and there was a weaver sitting at the loom, and the wife winding a clue of yarn.

"Tibby," quoth he, "what's that?"

"Oh," quoth she, "it's a wee bannock."

"It's well come," quoth he, "for our porrage were but thin to-day. Grip it, my woman; grip it."

"Ay," quoth she; "what recks! That's a clever bannock. Catch it, Willie; catch it, man."

"Hout," quoth Willie, "cast the clue at it."

But the bannock dodged round about, and off it went, and over the hill, like a new-tarred sheep or a mad cow. And forward it runs to the neat-house, to the fireside; and there was the goodwife churning.

"Come away, wee bannock," quoth she; "I'll have cream and bread to-day." But the wee bannock dodged round about the churn, and the wife after it, and in the hurry she had near-hand overturned the churn. And before she got it set right again, the wee bannock was off and down the brae to the mill; and in it ran.

The miller was sifting meal in the trough; but, looking up: "Ay," quoth he, "it's a sign of plenty when ye're running about, and nobody to look after ye. But I like a bannock and cheese. Come your way hither, and I'll give ye a night's quarters." But the bannock wouldn't trust itself with the miller and his cheese. So it turned and ran its way out; but the miller didn't fash his head with it.

So it toddled away and ran till it came to the smithy; and in it runs, and up to the anvil. The smith was making horse-nails. Quoth he: "I like a glass of good ale and a well-toasted bannock. Come your way in by here." But the bannock was frightened when it heard about the ale, and turned and was off as hard as it could, and the smith after it, and cast the hammer. But it missed, and the bannock was out of sight in a crack, and ran till it came to a farmhouse with a good peat-stack at the end of it. Inside it runs to the fireside. The goodman was cloving lint, and the goodwife heckling. "O Janet," quoth he, "there's a wee bannock; I'll have the half of it."

"Well, John, I'll have the other half. Hit it over the back with the clove." But the bannock played dodgings. "Hout, tout," quoth the wife, and made the heckle flee at it. But it was too clever for her.

And off and up the burn it ran to the next house, and rolled its way to the fireside. The goodwife was stirring the soup, and the goodman plaiting sprit-binnings for the cows. "Ho, Jock," quoth the goodwife, "here come. You're always crying about a wee bannock. Here's one. Come in, haste ye, and I'll help ye to grip it."

"Ay, mother, where is it?"

"See there. Run over on that side."

But the bannock ran in behind the goodman's chair. Jock fell among the sprits. The goodman cast a binning, and the goodwife the spurtle. But it was too clever for Jock and her both. It was off and out of sight in a crack, and through among the whins, and down the road to the next house, and in and snug by the fireside. The folk were just sitting down to their soup, and the goodwife scraping the pot. "Look," quoth she, "there's a wee bannock come in to warm itself at our fireside."

"Shut the door," quoth the goodman, "and we'll try to get a grip of it."

When the bannock heard that, it ran out of the house and they after it with their spoons, and the goodman shied his hat. But it rolled away and ran, and ran, till it came to another house; and when it went in the folk were just going to their beds. The goodman was taking off his breeches, and the goodwife raking the fire.

"What's that?" quoth he.

"Oh," quoth she, "it's a wee bannock."

Quoth he, "I could eat the half of it."

"Grip it," quoth the wife, "and I'll have a bit too."

"Cast your breeches at it!" The goodman shied his breeches, and had nearly smothered it. But it wriggled out and ran, and the goodman after it without his breeches; and there was a clean chase over the craft park, and in among the whins; and the goodman lost it, and had to come away, trotting home half naked. But now it was grown dark, and the wee bannock couldn't see; but it went into the side of a big whin bush, and into a fox's hole. The fox had had no meat for two days. "O welcome, welcome," quoth the fox, and snapped it in two in the middle. And that was the end of the wee bannock.

Johnny Gloke

Johnny Gloke was a tailor by trade, but like a man of spirit he grew tired of his tailoring, and wished to follow some other path that would lead to honour and fame. But he did not know what to do at first to gain fame and fortune, so for a time he was fonder of basking idly in the sun than in plying the needle and scissors. One warm day as he was enjoying his ease, he was annoyed by the flies alighting on his bare ankles. He brought his hand down on them with force and killed a goodly number of them. On counting the victims of his valour, he was overjoyed at his success; his heart rose to the doing of great deeds, and he gave vent to his feelings in the saying:—

"Well done! Johnny Gloke,
Kilt fifty flies at one stroke."

His resolution was now taken to cut out his path to fortune and honour. So he took down from its resting-place a rusty old sword that had belonged to some of his forebears, and set out in search of adventures. After travelling a long way, he came to a country that was much troubled by two giants, whom no one was bold enough to meet, and strong enough to overcome. He was soon told of the giants, and learned that the King of the country had offered a great reward and the hand of his daughter in marriage to the man who should rid his land of this scourge. John's heart rose to the deed, and he offered himself for the service. The great haunt of the giants was a wood, and John set out with his old sword to perform his task. When he reached the wood, he laid himself down to think what course he would follow, for he knew how weak he was compared to those he had undertaken to kill. He had not waited long, when he saw them coming with a waggon to fetch wood for fuel. My! they were big ones, with huge heads and long tusks for teeth. Johnny hid himself in the hollow of a tree, thinking only of his own safety. Feeling himself safe, he peeped out of his hiding-place, and watched the two at work. Thus watching he formed his plan of action. He picked up a pebble, threw it with force at one of them, and struck him a sharp blow on the head. The giant in his pain turned at once on his companion, and blamed him in strong words for hitting him. The other denied in anger that he had thrown the pebble. John now saw himself on the high way to gain his reward and the hand of the King's daughter. He kept still, and carefully watched for an opportunity of striking another blow. He soon found it, and right against the giant's head went another pebble. The injured giant fell on his companion in fury, and the two belaboured each other till they were utterly tired out. They sat down on a log to breathe, rest, and recover themselves.

While sitting, one of them said, "Well, all the King's army was not able to take us, but I fear an old woman with a rope's end would be too much for us now."

"If that be so," said Johnny Gloke, as he sprang, bold as a lion, from his hiding-place, "What do you say to Johnny Gloke with his old roosty sword?" So saying he fell upon them, cut off their heads, and returned in triumph. He received the King's daughter in marriage and for a time lived in peace and happiness. He never told the mode he followed in his dealing with the giants.

Some time after a rebellion broke out among the subjects of his father-in-law. John, on the strength of his former valiant deed, was chosen to quell the rebellion. His heart sank within him, but he could not refuse, and so lose his great name. He was mounted on the fiercest horse that ever saw sun or wind, and set out on his desperate task. He was not accustomed to ride on horseback, and he soon lost all control of his steed. It galloped off at full speed, in the direction of the rebel army. In its wild career it passed under the gallows that stood by the wayside. The gallows was somewhat old and frail, and down it fell on the horse's neck. Still the horse made no stop, but always forward at furious speed towards the rebels. On seeing this strange sight approaching towards them at such a speed they were seized with terror, and cried out to one another, "There comes Johnny Gloke that killed the two giants with the gallows on his horse's neck to hang us all." They broke their ranks, fled in dismay, and never stopped till they reached their homes. Thus was Johnny Gloke a second time victorious. So in due time he came to the throne and lived a long, happy, and good life as king.

Coat o' Clay

Once on a time, in the parts of Lindsey, there lived a wise woman. Some said she was a witch, but they said it in a whisper, lest she should overhear and do them a mischief, and truly it was not a thing one could be sure of, for she was never known to hurt any one, which, if she were a witch, she would have been sure to do. But she could tell you what your sickness was, and how to cure it with herbs, and she could mix rare possets that would drive the pain out of you in a twinkling; and she could advise you what to do if your cows were ill, or if you'd got into trouble, and tell the maids whether their sweethearts were likely to be faithful.

But she was ill-pleased if folks questioned her too much or too long, and she sore misliked fools. A many came to her asking foolish things, as was their nature, and to them she never gave counsel—at least of a kind that could aid them much.

Well, one day, as she sat at her door paring potatoes, over the stile and up the path came a tall lad with a long nose and goggle eyes and his hands in his pockets.

"That's a fool, if ever was one, and a fool's luck in his face," said the wise woman to herself with a nod of her head, and threw a potato skin over her left shoulder to keep off ill-chance.

"Good-day, missis," said the fool. "I be come to see thee."

"So thou art," said the wise woman; "I see that. How's all in thy folk this year?"

"Oh, fairly," answered he. "But they say I be a fool."

"Ay, so thou art," nodded she, and threw away a bad potato. "I see that too. But wouldst o' me? I keep no brains for sale."

"Well, see now. Mother says I'll ne'er be wiser all my born days; but folks tell us thou canst do everything. Can't thee teach me a bit, so they'll think me a clever fellow at home?"

"Hout-tout!" said the wise woman; "thou 'rt a bigger fool than I thought. Nay, I can't teach thee nought, lad; but I tell thee summat. Thou 'lt be a fool all thy days till thou gets a coat o' clay; and then thou 'lt know more than me."

"Hi, missis; what sort of a coat's that?" said he.

"That's none o' my business," answered she, "Thou 'st got to find out that."

And she took up her potatoes and went into her house.

The fool took off his cap and scratched his head.

"It's a queer kind of coat to look for, sure-*ly*," said he, "I never heard of a coat o' clay. But then I be a fool, that's true."

So he walked on till he came to the drain near by, with just a pickle of water and a foot of mud in it.

"Here's muck," said the fool, much pleased, and he got in and rolled in it spluttering. "Hi, yi!" said he—for he had his mouth full—"I've got a coat o' clay now to be sure. I'll go home and tell my mother I'm a wise man and not a fool any longer." And he went on home.

Presently he came to a cottage with a lass at the door.

"Morning, fool," said she; "hast thou been ducked in the horse-pond?"

"Fool yourself," said he, "the wise woman says I'll know more 'n she when I get a coat o' clay, and here it is. Shall I marry thee, lass?"

"Ay," said she, for she thought she'd like a fool for a husband, "when shall it be?"

"I'll come and fetch thee when I've told my mother," said the fool, and he gave her his lucky penny and went on.

When he got home his mother was on the doorstep.

"Mother, I 've got a coat o' clay," said he.

"Coat o' muck," said she; "and what of that?"

"Wise woman said I'd know more than she when I got a coat o' clay," said he, "so I down in the drain and got one, and I'm not a fool any longer."

"Very good," said his mother, "now thou canst get a wife."

"Ay," said he, "I'm going to marry so-an'-so."

"What!" said his mother, "*that* lass? No, and that thou 'lt not. She's nought but a brat, with ne'er a cow or a cabbage o' her own."

"But I gave her my luck penny," said the fool.

"Then thou 'rt a bigger fool than ever, for all thy coat o' clay!" said his mother, and banged the door in his face.

"Dang it!" said the fool, and scratched his head, "that's not the right sort o' clay sure-*ly*."

So back he went to the highroad and sat down on the bank of the river close by, looking at the water, which was cool and clear.

By-and-by he fell asleep, and before he knew what he was about—plump—he rolled off into the river with a splash, and scrambled out, dripping like a drowned rat.

"Dear, dear," said he, "I'd better go and get dry in the sun." So up he went to the highroad, and lay down in the dust, rolling about so that the sun should get at him all over.

Presently, when he sat up and looked down at himself, he found that the dust had caked into a sort of skin over his wet clothes till you could not see an inch of them, they were so well covered. "Hi, yi!" said he, "here's a coat o' clay ready made, and a fine one. See now, I'm a clever fellow this time sure-*ly*, for I've found what I wanted without looking for it! Wow, but it's a fine feeling to be so smart!"

And he sat and scratched his head, and thought about his own cleverness.

But all of a sudden, round the corner came the squire on horseback, full gallop, as if the boggles were after him; but the fool had to jump, even though the squire pulled his horse back on his haunches.

"What the dickens," said the squire, "do you mean by lying in the middle of the road like that?"

"Well, master," said the fool, "I fell into the water and got wet, so I lay down in the road to get dry; and I lay down a fool an' got up a wise man."

"How's that?" said the squire.

So the fool told him about the wise woman and the coat o' clay.

"Ah, ah!" laughed the squire, "whoever heard of a wise man lying in the middle of the highroad to be ridden over? Lad, take my word for it, you are a bigger fool than ever," and he rode on laughing.

"Dang it!" said the fool, as he scratched his head. "I've not got the right sort of coat yet, then." And he choked and spluttered in the dust that the squire's horse had raised.

So on he went in a melancholy mood till he came to an inn, and the landlord at his door smoking.

"Well, fool," said he, "thou 'rt fine and dirty."

"Ay," said the fool, "I be dirty outside an' dusty in, but it's not the right thing yet."

And he told the landlord all about the wise woman and the coat o' clay.

"Hout-tout!" said the landlord, with a wink. "I know what's wrong. Thou 'st got a skin o' dirt outside and all dry dust inside. Thou must moisten it, lad, with a good drink, and then thou 'lt have a real all-over coat o' clay."

"Hi," said the fool, "that's a good word."

So down he sat and began to drink. But it was wonderful how much liquor it took to moisten so much dust; and each time he got to the bottom of the pot he found he was still dry. At last he began to feel very merry and pleased with himself.

"Hi, yi!" said he. "I've got a real coat o' clay now outside and in—what a difference it do make, to be sure. I feel another man now—so smart."

And he told the landlord he was certainly a wise man now, though he couldn't speak over-distinctly after drinking so much. So up he got, and thought he would go home and tell his mother she hadn't a fool for a son any more.

But just as he was trying to get through the inn-door which would scarcely keep still long enough for him to find it, up came the landlord and caught him by the sleeve.

"See here, master," said he, "thou hasn't paid for thy score—where's thy money?"

"Haven't any!" said the fool, and pulled out his pockets to show they were empty.

"What!" said the landlord, and swore; "thou 'st drunk all my liquor and haven't got nought to pay for it with!"

"Hi!" said the fool. "You told me to drink so as to get a coat o' clay; but as I'm a wise man now I don't mind helping thee along in the world a bit, for though I'm a smart fellow I'm not too proud to my friends."

"Wise man! smart fellow!" said the landlord, "and help me along, wilt thee? Dang it! thou 'rt the biggest fool I ever saw, and it's I'll help *thee* first—out o' this!"

And he kicked him out of the door into the road and swore at him.

"Hum," said the fool, as he lay in the dust, "I'm not so wise as I thought. I guess I'll go back to the wise woman and tell her there's a screw loose somewhere."

So up he got and went along to her house, and found her sitting at the door.

"So thou 'rt come back," said she, with a nod. "What dost thou want with me now?"

So he sat down and told her how he'd tried to get a coat o' clay, and he wasn't any wiser for all of it.

"No," said the wise woman, "thou 'rt a bigger fool than ever, my lad."

"So they all say," sighed the fool; "but where can I get the right sort of coat o' clay, then, missis?"

"When thou 'rt done with this world, and thy folk put thee in the ground," said the wise woman. "That's the only coat o' clay as 'll make such as *thee* wise, lad. Born a fool, die a fool, and be a fool thy life long, and that's the truth!"

And she went into the house and shut the door.

"Dang it," said the fool. "I must tell my mother she was right after all, and that she'll never have a wise man for a son!"

And he went off home.

The Three Cows

There was a farmer, and he had three cows, fine fat beauties they were. One was called Facey, the other Diamond, and the third Beauty. One morning he went into his cowshed, and there he found Facey so thin that the wind would have blown her away. Her skin hung loose about her, all her flesh was gone, and she stared out of her great eyes as though she'd seen a ghost; and what was more, the fireplace in the kitchen was one great pile of wood-ash. Well, he was bothered with it; he could not see how all this had come about.

Next morning his wife went out to the shed, and see! Diamond was for all the world as wisht a looking creature as Facey—nothing but a bag of bones, all the flesh gone, and half a rick of wood was gone too; but the fireplace was piled up three feet high with white wood-ashes. The farmer determined to watch the third night; so he hid in a closet which opened out of the parlour, and he left the door just ajar, that he might see what passed.

Tick, tick, went the clock, and the farmer was nearly tired of waiting; he had to bite his little finger to keep himself awake, when suddenly the door of his house flew open, and in rushed maybe a thousand pixies, laughing and dancing and dragging at Beauty's halter till they had brought the cow into the middle of the room. The farmer really thought he should have died with fright, and so perhaps he would had not curiosity kept him alive.

Tick, tick, went the clock, but he did not hear it now. He was too intent staring at the pixies and his last beautiful cow. He saw them throw her down, fall on her, and kill her; then with their knives they ripped her open, and flayed her as clean as a whistle. Then out ran some of the little people and brought in firewood and made a roaring blaze on the hearth, and there they cooked the flesh of the cow—they baked and they boiled, they stewed and they fried.

"Take care," cried one, who seemed to be the king, "let no bone be broken."

Well, when they had all eaten, and had devoured every scrap of beef on the cow, they began playing games with the bones, tossing them one to another. One little leg-bone fell close to the closet door, and the farmer was so afraid lest the pixies should come there and find him in their search for the bone, that he put out his hand and drew it in to him. Then he saw the king stand on the table and say, "Gather the bones!"

Round and round flew the imps, picking up the bones. "Arrange them," said the king; and they placed them all in their proper positions in the hide of the cow. Then they folded the skin over them, and the king struck the heap of bone and skin with his rod. Whisht! up sprang the cow and lowed dismally. It was alive again; but, alas! as the pixies dragged it back to its stall, it halted in the off forefoot, for a bone was missing.

"The cock crew,
Away they flew."

and the farmer crept trembling to bed.

The Blinded Giant

At Dalton, near Thirsk, in Yorkshire, there is a mill. It has quite recently been rebuilt; but when I was at Dalton, six years ago, the old building stood. In front of the house was a long mound which went by the name of "the giant's grave," and in the mill you can see a long blade of iron something like a scythe-blade, but not curved, which was called "the giant's knife," because of a very curious story which is told of this knife. Would you like to hear it? Well, it isn't very long.

There once lived a giant at this mill who had only one eye in the middle of his forehead, and he ground men's bones to make his bread. One day he captured on Pilmoor a lad named Jack, and instead of grinding him in the mill he kept him grinding as his servant, and never let him get away. Jack served the giant seven years, and never was allowed a holiday the whole time. At last he could bear it no longer. Topcliffe fair was coming on, and Jack begged that he might be allowed to go there.

"No, no," said the giant, "stop at home and mind your grinding."

"I've been grinding and grinding these seven years," said Jack, "and not a holiday have I had. I'll have one now, whatever you say."

"We'll see about that," said the giant.

Well, the day was hot, and after dinner the giant lay down in the mill with his head on a sack and dozed. He had been eating in the mill, and had laid down a great loaf of bone bread by his side, and the knife I told you about was in his hand, but his fingers relaxed their hold of it in sleep. Jack seized the knife, and holding it with both his hands drove the blade into the single eye of the giant, who woke with a howl of agony, and starting up, barred the door. Jack was again in difficulties, for he couldn't get out, but he soon found a way out of them. The giant had a favourite dog, which had also been sleeping when his master was blinded. So Jack killed the dog, skinned it, and threw the hide over his back.

"Bow, wow," says Jack.

"At him, Truncheon," said the giant; "at the little wretch that I've fed these seven years, and now has blinded me."

"Bow, wow," says Jack, and ran between the giant's legs on all-fours, barking till he got to the door. He unlatched it and was off, and never more was seen at Dalton Mill.

Scrapefoot

Once upon a time, there were three Bears who lived in a castle in a great wood. One of them was a great big Bear, and one was a middling Bear, and one was a little Bear. And in the same wood there was a Fox who lived all alone, his name was Scrapefoot. Scrapefoot was very much afraid of the Bears, but for all that he wanted very much to know all about them. And one day as he went through the wood he found himself near the Bears' Castle, and he wondered whether he could get into the castle. He looked all about him everywhere, and he could not see any one. So he came up very quietly, till at last he came up to the door of the castle, and he tried whether he could open it. Yes! the door was not locked, and he opened it just a little way, and put his nose in and looked, and he could not see any one. So then he opened it a little way farther, and put one paw in, and then another paw, and another and another, and then he was all in the Bears' Castle. He found he was in a great hall with three chairs in it—one big, one middling, and one little chair; and he thought he would like to sit down and rest and look about him; so he sat down on the big chair. But he found it so hard and uncomfortable that it made his bones ache, and he jumped down at once and got into the middling chair, and he turned round and round in it, but he couldn't make himself comfortable. So then he went to the little chair and sat down in it, and it was so soft and warm and comfortable that Scrapefoot was quite happy; but all at once it broke to pieces under him and he couldn't put it together again! So he got up and began to look about him again, and on one table he saw three saucers, of which one was very big, one was middling, one was quite a little saucer. Scrapefoot was very thirsty, and he began to drink out of the big saucer. But he only just tasted the milk in the big saucer, which was so sour and so nasty that he would not taste another drop of it. Then he tried the middling saucer, and he drank a little of that. He tried two or three mouthfuls, but it was not nice, and then he left it and went to the little saucer, and the milk in the little saucer was so sweet and so nice that he went on drinking it till it was all gone.

Then Scrapefoot thought he would like to go upstairs; and he listened and he could not hear any one. So upstairs he went, and he found a great room with three beds in it; one was a big bed, and one was a middling bed, and one was a little white bed; and he climbed up into the big bed, but it was so hard and lumpy and uncomfortable that he jumped down again at once, and tried the middling bed. That was rather better, but he could not get comfortably in it, so after turning about a little while he got up and went to the little bed; and that was so soft and so warm and so nice that he fell fast asleep at once.

And after a time the Bears came home, and when they got into the hall the big Bear went to his chair and said, "WHO'S BEEN SITTING IN MY CHAIR?" and the middling Bear said, "WHO'S BEEN SITTING IN MY CHAIR?" and the little Bear said, "*Who's been sitting in my chair and has broken it all to pieces?*" And then they went to have their milk, and the big Bear said, "WHO'S BEEN DRINKING MY MILK?" and the middling Bear said, "WHO'S BEEN DRINKING MY MILK?" and the little Bear said, "*Who's been drinking my milk and has drunk it all up?*" Then they went upstairs and into the bedroom, and the big Bear said, "WHO'S BEEN SLEEPING IN MY BED?" and the middling Bear said, "WHO'S BEEN SLEEPING IN MY BED?" and the little Bear said, "*Who's been sleeping in my bed?—and see here he is!*" So then the Bears came and wondered what they should do with him; and the big Bear said, "Let's hang him!" and then the middling Bear said, "Let's drown him!" and then the little Bear said, "Let's throw him out of the window." And then the Bears took him to the window, and the big Bear took two legs on one side and the middling Bear took two legs on the other side, and they swung him backwards and forwards, backwards and forwards, and out of the window. Poor Scrapefoot was so frightened, and he thought every bone in his body must be broken. But he got up and first shook one leg—no, that was not broken; and then another, and that was not broken; and another and another, and then he wagged his tail and found there were no bones broken. So then he galloped off home as fast as he could go, and never went near the Bears' Castle again.

The Pedlar of Swaffham

In the old days when London Bridge was lined with shops from one end to the other, and salmon swam under the arches, there lived at Swaffham, in Norfolk, a poor pedlar. He'd much ado to make his living, trudging about with his pack at his back and his dog at his heels, and at the close of the day's labour was but too glad to sit down and sleep. Now it fell out that one night he dreamed a dream, and therein he saw the great bridge of London town, and it sounded in his ears that if he went there he should hear joyful news. He made little count of the dream, but on the following night it come back to him, and again on the third night.

Then he said within himself, "I must needs try the issue of it," and so he trudged up to London town. Long was the way and right glad was he when he stood on the great bridge and saw the tall houses on right hand and left, and had glimpses of the water running and the ships sailing by. All day long he paced to and fro, but he heard nothing that might yield him comfort. And again on the morrow he stood and he gazed—he paced afresh the length of London Bridge, but naught did he see and naught did he hear.

Now the third day being come as he still stood and gazed, a shopkeeper hard by spoke to him.

"Friend," said he, "I wonder much at your fruitless standing. Have you no wares to sell?"

"No, indeed," quoth the pedlar.

"And you do not beg for alms."

"Not so long as I can keep myself."

"Then what, I pray thee, dost thou want here, and what may thy business be?"

"Well, kind sir, to tell the truth, I dreamed that if I came hither, I should hear good news."

Right heartily did the shopkeeper laugh.

"Nay, thou must be a fool to take a journey on such a silly errand. I'll tell thee, poor silly country fellow, that I myself dream too o' nights, and that last night I dreamt myself to be in Swaffham, a place clean unknown to me, but in Norfolk if I mistake not, and methought I was in an orchard behind a pedlar's house, and in that orchard was a great oak-tree. Then meseemed that if I digged I should find beneath that tree a great treasure. But think you I'm such a fool as to take on me a long and wearisome journey and all for a silly dream. No, my good fellow, learn wit from a wiser man than thyself. Get thee home, and mind thy business."

When the pedlar heard this he spoke no word, but was exceeding glad in himself, and returning home speedily, digged underneath the great oak-tree, and found a prodigious great treasure. He grew exceeding rich, but he did not forget his duty in the pride of his riches. For he built up again the church at Swaffham, and when he died they put a statue of him therein all in stone with his pack at his back and his dog at his heels. And there it stands to this day to witness if I lie.

The Old Witch

Once upon a time there were two girls who lived with their mother and father. Their father had no work, and the girls wanted to go away and seek their fortunes. Now one girl wanted to go to service, and her mother said she might if she could find a place. So she started for the town. Well, she went all about the town, but no one wanted a girl like her. So she went on farther into the country, and she came to the place where there was an oven where there was lots of bread baking. And the bread said, "Little girl, little girl, take us out, take us out. We have been baking seven years, and no one has come to take us out." So the girl took out the bread, laid it on the ground, and went on her way. Then she met a cow, and the cow said, "Little girl, little girl, milk me, milk me! Seven years have I been waiting, and no one has come to milk me." The girl milked the cow into the pails that stood by. As she was thirsty she drank some, and left the rest in the pails by the cow. Then she went on a little bit farther, and came to an apple tree, so loaded with fruit that its branches were breaking down, and the tree said, "Little girl, little girl, help me shake my fruit. My branches are breaking, it is so heavy." And the girl said, "Of course I will, you poor tree." So she shook the fruit all off, propped up the branches, and left the fruit on the ground under the tree. Then she went on again till she came to a house. Now in this house there lived a witch, and this witch took girls into her house as servants. And when she heard that this girl had left her home to seek service, she said that she would try her, and give her good wages. The witch told the girl what work she was to do. "You must keep the house clean and tidy, sweep the floor and the fireplace; but there is one thing you must never do. You must never look up the chimney, or something bad will befall you."

So the girl promised to do as she was told, but one morning as she was cleaning, and the witch was out, she forgot what the witch said, and looked up the chimney. When she did this a great bag of money fell down in her lap. This happened again and again. So the girl started to go off home.

When she had gone some way she heard the witch coming after her. So she ran to the apple tree and cried:

"Apple-tree, apple-tree hide me,
So the old witch can't find me;
If she does she'll pick my bones,
And bury me under the marble stones."

So the apple-tree hid her. When the witch came up she said:

"Tree of mine, tree of mine,
Have you seen a girl
With a willy-willy wag, and a long-tailed bag,
Who stole my money, all I had?"

"Tree of mine, tree of mine,
Have you seen a girl
With a willy-willy wag, and a long-tailed bag,
Who's stole my money, all I had?"

And the apple-tree said, "No, mother; not for seven year."

When the witch had gone down another way, the girl went on again, and just as she got to the cow heard the witch coming after her again, so she ran to the cow and cried:

"Cow, cow, hide me,
So the old witch can't find me;
If she does she'll pick my bones,
And bury me under the marble stones."

So the cow hid her.

When the old witch came up, she looked about and said to the cow:

"Cow of mine, cow of mine,
Have you seen a girl
With a willy-willy wag, and a long-tailed bag,
Who's stole my money, all I had?"

And the cow said, "No, mother, not for seven year."

When the witch had gone off another way, the little girl went on again, and when she was near the oven she heard the witch coming after her again, so she ran to the oven and cried:

"Oven, oven, hide me,
So the old witch can't find me;
If she does she'll break my bones,
And bury me under the marble stones."

And the oven said, "I've no room, ask the baker," and the baker hid her behind the oven.

When the witch came up she looked here and there and everywhere, and then said to the baker:

"Man of mine, man of mine,
Have you seen a girl,
With a willy-willy wag, and a long-tailed bag,
Who's stole my money, all I had?"

So the baker said, "Look in the oven." The old witch went to look, and the oven said, "Get in and look in the furthest corner." The witch did so, and when she was inside the oven shut her door, and the witch was kept there for a very long time.

The girl then went off again, and reached her home with her money bags, married a rich man, and lived happy ever afterwards.

The other sister then thought she would go and do the same. And she went the same way. But when she reached the oven, and the bread said, "Little girl, little girl, take us out. Seven years have we been baking, and no one has come to take us out," the girl said, "No, I don't want to burn my fingers." So she went on till she met the cow, and the cow said, "Little girl, little girl, milk me, milk me, do. Seven years have I been waiting, and no one has come to milk me." But the girl said, "No, I can't milk you, I'm in a hurry," and went on faster. Then she came to the apple-tree, and the apple-tree asked her to help shake the fruit. "No, I can't; another day p'raps I may," and went on till she came to the witch's house. Well, it happened to her just the same as to the other girl—she forgot what she was told, and one day when the witch was out, looked up the chimney, and down fell a bag of money. Well, she thought she would be off at once. When she reached the apple-tree, she heard the witch coming after her, and she cried:

"Apple-tree, apple-tree, hide me,
So the old witch can't find me;
If she does she'll break my bones,
And bury me under the marble stones."

But the tree didn't answer, and she ran on further. Presently the witch came up and said:

"Tree of mine, tree of mine,
Have you seen a girl,
With a willy-willy wag, and a long-tailed bag,
Who's stole my money, all I had?"

The tree said, "Yes, mother; she's gone down that way."

So the old witch went after her and caught her, she took all the money away from her, beat her, and sent her off home just as she was.

The Three Wishes

Once upon a time, and be sure 't was a long time ago, there lived a poor woodman in a great forest, and every day of his life he went out to fell timber. So one day he started out, and the goodwife filled his wallet and slung his bottle on his back, that he might have meat and drink in the forest. He had marked out a huge old oak, which, thought he, would furnish many and many a good plank. And when he was come to it, he took his axe in his hand and swung it round his head as though he were minded to fell the tree at one stroke. But he hadn't given one blow, when what should he hear but the pitifullest entreating, and there stood before him a fairy who prayed and beseeched him to spare the tree. He was dazed, as you may fancy, with wonderment and affright, and he couldn't open his mouth to utter a word. But he found his tongue at last, and, "Well," said he, "I'll e'en do as thou wishest."

"You've done better for yourself than you know," answered the fairy, "and to show I'm not ungrateful, I'll grant you your next three wishes, be they what they may." And therewith the fairy was no more to be seen, and the woodman slung his wallet over his shoulder and his bottle at his side, and off he started home.

But the way was long, and the poor man was regularly dazed with the wonderful thing that had befallen him, and when he got home there was nothing in his noddle but the wish to sit down and rest. Maybe, too, 't was a trick of the fairy's. Who can tell? Anyhow down he sat by the blazing fire, and as he sat he waxed hungry, though it was a long way off supper-time yet.

"Hasn't thou naught for supper, dame?" said he to his wife.

"Nay, not for a couple of hours yet," said she.

"Ah!" groaned the woodman, "I wish I'd a good link of black pudding here before me."

No sooner had he said the word, when clatter, clatter, rustle, rustle, what should come down the chimney but a link of the finest black pudding the heart of man could wish for.

If the woodman stared, the goodwife stared three times as much. "What's all this?" says she.

Then all the morning's work came back to the woodman, and he told his tale right out, from beginning to end, and as he told it the goodwife glowered and glowered, and when he had made an end of it she burst out, "Thou bee'st but a fool, Jan, thou bee'st but a fool; and I wish the pudding were at thy nose, I do indeed."

And before you could say Jack Robinson, there the goodman sat and his nose was the longer for a noble link of black pudding.

He gave a pull but it stuck, and she gave a pull but it stuck, and they both pulled till they had nigh pulled the nose off, but it stuck and stuck.

"What's to be done now?" said he.

"'T isn't so very unsightly," said she, looking hard at him.

Then the woodman saw that if he wished, he must need wish in a hurry; and wish he did, that the black pudding might come off his nose. Well! there it lay in a dish on the table, and if the goodman and goodwife didn't ride in a golden coach, or dress in silk and satin, why, they had at least as fine a black pudding for their supper as the heart of man could desire.

The Buried Moon

Long ago, in my grandmother's time, the Carland was all in bogs, great pools of black water, and creeping trickles of green water, and squishy mools which squirted when you stepped on them.

Well, granny used to say how long before her time the Moon herself was once dead and buried in the marshes, and as she used to tell me, I'll tell you all about it.

The Moon up yonder shone and shone, just as she does now, and when she shone she lighted up the bog-pools, so that one could walk about almost as safe as in the day.

But when she didn't shine, out came the Things that dwelt in the darkness and went about seeking to do evil and harm; Bogles and Crawling Horrors, all came out when the Moon didn't shine.

Well, the Moon heard of this, and being kind and good—as she surely is, shining for us in the night instead of taking her natural rest—she was main troubled. "I'll see for myself, I will," said she, "maybe it's not so bad as folks make out."

Sure enough, at the month's end down she stept, wrapped up in a black cloak, and a black hood over her yellow shining hair. Straight she went to the bog edge and looked about her. Water here and water there; waving tussocks and trembling mools, and great black snags all twisted and bent. Before her all was dark—dark but for the glimmer of the stars in the pools, and the light that came from her own white feet, stealing out of her black cloak.

The Moon drew her cloak faster about and trembled, but she wouldn't go back without seeing all there was to be seen; so on she went, stepping as light as the wind in summer from tuft to tuft between the greedy gurgling water holes. Just as she came near a big black pool her foot slipped and she was nigh tumbling in. She grabbed with both hands at a snag near by to steady herself with, but as she touched it, it twined itself round her wrists, like a pair of handcuffs, and gript her so that she couldn't move. She pulled and twisted and fought, but it was no good. She was fast, and must stay fast.

Presently as she stood trembling in the dark, wondering if help would come, she heard something calling in the distance, calling, calling, and then dying away with a sob, till the marshes were full of this pitiful crying sound; then she heard steps floundering along, squishing in the mud and slipping on the tufts, and through the darkness she saw a white face with great feared eyes.

'T was a man strayed in the bogs. Mazed with fear he struggled on toward the flickering light that looked like help and safety. And when the poor Moon saw that he was coming nigher and nigher to the deep hole, further and further from the path, she was so mad and so sorry that she struggled and fought and pulled harder than ever. And though she couldn't get loose, she twisted and turned, till her black hood fell back off her shining yellow hair, and the beautiful light that came from it drove away the darkness.

Oh, but the man cried with joy to see the light again. And at once all evil things fled back into the dark corners, for they cannot abide the light. So he could see where he was, and where the path was, and how he could get out of the marsh. And he was in such haste to get away from the Quicks, and Bogles, and Things that dwelt there, that he scarce looked at the brave light that came from the beautiful shining yellow hair, streaming out over the black cloak and falling to the water at his feet. And the Moon herself was so taken up with saving him, and with rejoicing that he was back on the right path, that she clean forgot that she needed help herself, and that she was held fast by the Black Snag.

So off he went; spent and gasping, and stumbling and sobbing with joy, flying for his life out of the terrible bogs. Then it came over the Moon, she would main like to go with him. So she pulled and fought as if she were mad, till she fell on her knees, spent with tugging, at the foot of the snag. And as she lay there, gasping for breath, the black hood fell forward over her head. So out went the blessed light and back came the darkness, with all its Evil Things, with a screech and a howl. They came crowding round her, mocking and snatching and beating; shrieking with rage and spite, and swearing and snarling, for they knew her for their old enemy, that drove them back into the corners, and kept them from working their wicked wills.

"Drat thee!" yelled the witch-bodies, "thou 'st spoiled our spells this year agone!"

"And us thou sent'st to brood in the corners!" howled the Bogles.

And all the Things joined in with a great "Ho, ho!" till the very tussocks shook and the water gurgled. And they began again.

"We'll poison her—poison her!" shrieked the witches.

And "Ho, ho!" howled the Things again.

"We'll smother her—smother her!" whispered the Crawling Horrors, and twined themselves round her knees.

And "Ho, ho!" mocked the rest of them.

And again they all shouted with spite and ill-will. And the poor Moon crouched down, and wished she was dead and done with.

And they fought and squabbled what they should do with her, till a pale grey light began to come in the sky; and it drew nigh the dawning. And when they saw that, they were feared lest they shouldn't have time to work their will; and they caught hold of her, with horrid bony fingers, and laid her deep in the water at the foot of the snag. And the Bogles fetched a strange big stone and rolled it on top of her, to keep her from rising. And they told two of the Will-o-the-wykes to take turns in watching on the black snag, to see that she lay safe and still, and couldn't get out to spoil their sport.

And there lay the poor Moon, dead and buried in the bog, till some one would set her loose; and who'd know where to look for her.

Well, the days passed, and 't was the time for the new moon's coming, and the folk put pennies in their pockets and straws in their caps so as to be ready for her, and looked about, for the Moon was a good friend to the marsh folk, and they were main glad when the dark time was gone, and the paths were safe again, and the Evil Things were driven back by the blessed Light into the darkness and the waterholes.

But days and days passed, and the new Moon never came, and the nights were aye dark, and the Evil Things were worse than ever. And still the days went on, and the new Moon never came. Naturally the poor folk were strangely feared and mazed, and a lot of them went to the Wise Woman who dwelt in the old mill, and asked if so be she could find out where the Moon was gone.

"Well," said she, after looking in the brewpot, and in the mirror, and in the Book, "it be main queer, but I can't rightly tell ye what's happened to her. If ye hear of aught, come and tell me."

So they went their ways; and as days went by, and never a Moon came, naturally they talked—my word! I reckon they *did* talk! their tongues wagged at home, and at the inn, and in the garth. But so came one day, as they sat on the great settle in the Inn, a man from the far end of the bog lands was smoking and listening, when all at once he sat up and slapped his knee. "My faicks!" says he, "I'd clean forgot, but I reckon I kens where the Moon be!" and he told them of how he was lost in the bogs, and how, when he was nigh dead with fright, the light shone out, and he found the path and got home safe.

So off they all went to the Wise Woman, and told her about it, and she looked long in the pot and the Book again, and then she nodded her head.

"It's dark still, childer, dark!" says she, "and I can't rightly see, but do as I tell ye, and ye 'll find out for yourselves. Go all of ye, just afore the night gathers, put a stone in your mouth, and take a hazel-twig in your hands, and say never a word till you're safe home again. Then walk on and fear not, far into the midst of the marsh, till ye find a coffin, a candle, and a cross. Then ye'll not be far from your Moon; look, and m'appen ye 'll find her."

So came the next night in the darklings, out they went all together, every man with a stone in his mouth, and a hazel-twig in his hand, and feeling, thou may'st reckon, main feared and creepy. And they stumbled and stottered along the paths into the midst of the bogs; they saw nought, though they heard sighings and flutterings in their ears, and felt cold wet fingers touching them; but all at once, looking around for the coffin, the candle, and the cross, while they came nigh to the pool beside the great snag, where the Moon lay buried. And all at once they stopped, quaking and mazed and skeery, for there was the great stone, half in, half out of the water, for all the world like a strange big coffin; and at the head was the black snag, stretching out its two arms in a dark gruesome cross, and on it a tiddy light flickered, like a dying candle. And they all knelt down in the mud, and said, "Our Lord, first forward, because of the cross, and then backward, to keep off the Bogles; but without speaking out, for they knew that the Evil Things would catch them, if they didn't do as the Wise Woman told them."

Then they went nigher, and took hold of the big stone, and shoved it up, and afterwards they said that for one tiddy minute they saw a strange and beautiful face looking up at them glad-like out of the black water; but the Light came so quick and so white and shining, that they stept back mazed with it, and the very next minute, when they could see again, there was the full Moon in the sky, bright and beautiful and kind as ever, shining and smiling down at them, and making the bogs and the paths as clear as day, and stealing into the very corners, as though she'd have driven the darkness and the Bogles clean away if she could.

A Son of Adam

A man was one day working. It was very hot, and he was digging. By-and-by he stopped to rest and wipe his face; and he was very angry to think he had to work so hard only because of Adam's sin. So he complained bitterly, and said some very hard words about Adam.

It happened that his master heard him, and he asked, "Why do you blame Adam? You'd ha' done just like Adam, if you'd a-been in his place."

"No, I shouldn't," said the man; "I should ha' know'd better."

"Well, I'll try you," says his master; "come to me at dinner-time."

So come dinner-time, the man came, and his master took him into a room where the table was a-set with good things of all sorts. And he said: "Now, you can eat as much as ever you like from any of the dishes on the table; but don't touch the covered dish in the middle till I come back." And with that the master went out of the room and left the man there all by himself.

So the man sat down and helped himself, and ate some o' this dish and some o' that, and enjoyed himself finely. But after awhile, as his master didn't come back, he began to look at the covered dish, and to wonder whatever was in it. And he wondered more and more, and he says to himself, "It must be something very nice. Why shouldn't I just look at it? I won't touch it. There can't be any harm in just peeping." So at last he could hold back no longer, and he lifted up the cover a tiny bit; but he couldn't see anything. Then he lifted it up a bit more, and out popped a mouse. The man tried to catch it; but it ran away and jumped off the table and he ran after it. It ran first into one corner, and then, just as he thought he'd got it, into another, and under the table, and all about the room. And the man made such a clatter, jumping and banging and running round after the mouse, a-trying to catch it, that at last his master came in.

"Ah!" he said; "never you blame Adam again, my man!"

The Children in the Wood

Now ponder well, you parents dear,
These words which I shall write;
A doleful story you shall hear,
In time brought forth to light.
A gentleman of good account,
In Norfolk dwelt of late,
Who did in honour far surmount
Most men of his estate.

Sore sick he was and like to die,
No help his life could save;
His wife by him as sick did lie,
And both possest one grave.
No love between these two was lost,
Each was to other kind;
In love they lived, in love they died,
And left two babes behind.

The one a fine and pretty boy
Not passing three years old,
The other a girl more young than he,
And framed in beauty's mould.
The father left his little son,
As plainly did appear,
When he to perfect age should come,
Three hundred pounds a year;

And to his little daughter Jane
Five hundred pounds in gold,
To be paid down on marriage-day,
Which might not be controlled.
But if the children chanced to die
Ere they to age should come,
Their uncle should possess their wealth;
For so the will did run.

"Now, brother," said the dying man,
"Look to my children dear;
Be good unto my boy and girl,
No friends else have they here;
To God and you I recommend
My children dear this day;
But little while be sure we have

Within this world to stay.

"You must be father and mother both,
And uncle, all in one;
God knows what will become of them
When I am dead and gone."
With that bespake their mother dear:
"O brother kind," quoth she,
"You are the man must bring our babes
To wealth or misery.

"And if you keep them carefully,
Then God will you reward;
But if you otherwise should deal,
God will your deeds regard."
With lips as cold as any stone,
They kissed their children small:
"God bless you both, my children dear!"
With that the tears did fall.

These speeches then their brother spake
To this sick couple there:
"The keeping of your little ones,
Sweet sister, do not fear;
God never prosper me nor mine,
Nor aught else that I have,
If I do wrong your children dear
When you are laid in grave!"

The parents being dead and gone,
The children home he takes,
And brings them straight unto his house
Where much of them he makes.
He had not kept these pretty babes
A twelvemonth and a day,
But, for their wealth, he did devise
To make them both away.

He bargained with two ruffians strong,
Which were of furious mood,
That they should take these children young,
And slay them in a wood.
He told his wife an artful tale
He would the children send
To be brought up in London town
With one that was his friend.

Away then went those pretty babes,
Rejoicing at that tide,
Rejoicing with a merry mind
They should on cock-horse ride.
They prate and prattle pleasantly,
As they ride on the way,
To those that should their butchers be
And work their lives' decay:

So that the pretty speech they had
Made Murder's heart relent;
And they that undertook the deed
Full sore now did repent.
Yet one of them, more hard of heart,
Did vow to do his charge,
Because the wretch that hired him
Had paid him very large.

The other won't agree thereto,
So there they fall to strife;
With one another they did fight
About the children's life;
And he that was of mildest mood
Did slay the other there,
Within an unfrequented wood;
The babes did quake for fear!

He took the children by the hand,
Tears standing in their eye,
And bade them straightway follow him,
And look they did not cry;
And two long miles he led them on,
While they for food complain:
"Stay here," quoth he, "I'll bring you bread,
When I come back again."

These pretty babes, with hand in hand,
Went wandering up and down;
But never more could see the man
Approaching from the town.
Their pretty lips with blackberries
Were all besmeared and dyed;
And when they saw the darksome night,
They sat them down and cried.

Thus wandered these poor innocents,
Till death did end their grief;
In one another's arms they died,
As wanting due relief:
No burial this pretty pair
From any man receives,
Till Robin Redbreast piously
Did cover them with leaves.

And now the heavy wrath of God
Upon their uncle fell;
Yea, fearful fiends did haunt his house,
His conscience felt an hell:
His barns were fired, his goods consumed,
His lands were barren made,
His cattle died within the field,
And nothing with him stayed.

And in a voyage to Portugal
Two of his sons did die;
And to conclude, himself was brought
To want and misery:
He pawned and mortgaged all his land
Ere seven years came about.
And now at last this wicked act
Did by this means come out,

The fellow that did take in hand
These children for to kill,
Was for a robbery judged to die,
Such was God's blessèd will:
Who did confess the very truth,
As here hath been displayed:
The uncle having died in jail,
Where he for debt was laid.

You that executors be made,
And overseers eke,
Of children that be fatherless,
And infants mild and meek,
Take you example by this thing,
And yield to each his right,
Lest God with suchlike misery
Your wicked minds requite.

The Hobyahs

Once there was an old man and woman and a little girl, and they all lived in a house made of hempstalks. Now the old man had a little dog named Turpie; and one night the Hobyahs came and said, "Hobyah! Hobyah! Hobyah! Tear down the hempstalks, eat up the old man and woman, and carry off the little girl!" But little dog Turpie barked so that the Hobyahs ran off; and the old man said, "Little dog Turpie barks so that I cannot sleep nor slumber, and if I live till morning I will cut off his tail." So in the morning the old man cut off little dog Turpie's tail.

The next night the Hobyahs came again, and said, "Hobyah! Hobyah! Hobyah! Tear down the hempstalks, eat up the old man and woman, and carry off the little girl!" But little dog Turpie barked so that the Hobyahs ran off; and the old man said, "Little dog Turpie barks so that I cannot sleep nor slumber, and if I live till morning I will cut off one of his legs." So in the morning the old man cut off one of little dog Turpie's legs.

The next night the Hobyahs came again, and said, "Hobyah! Hobyah! Hobyah! Tear down the hempstalks, eat up the old man and woman, and carry off the little girl!" But little dog Turpie barked so that the Hobyahs ran off; and the old man said, "Little dog

Turpie barks so that I cannot sleep nor slumber, and if I live till morning I will cut off another of his legs." So in the morning the old man cut off another of little dog Turpie's legs.

The next night the Hobyahs came again, and said, "Hobyah! Hobyah! Hobyah! Tear down the hempstalks, eat up the old man and woman, and carry off the little girl!" But little dog Turpie barked so that the Hobyahs ran off; and the old man said, "Little dog Turpie barks so that I cannot sleep nor slumber, and if I live till morning I will cut off another of his legs." So in the morning the old man cut off another of little dog Turpie's legs.

The next night the Hobyahs came again, and said, "Hobyah! Hobyah! Hobyah! Tear down the hempstalks, eat up the old man and woman, and carry off the little girl!" But little dog Turpie barked so that the Hobyahs ran off; and the old man said, "Little dog Turpie barks so that I cannot sleep nor slumber, and if I live till morning I will cut off another of his legs." So in the morning the old man cut off another of little dog Turpie's legs.

The next night the Hobyahs came again, and said, "Hobyah! Hobyah! Hobyah! Tear down the hempstalks, eat up the old man and woman, and carry off the little girl!" But little dog Turpie barked so that the Hobyahs ran off; and the old man said, "Little dog Turpie barks so that I cannot sleep nor slumber, and if I live till morning I will cut off little dog Turpie's head." So in the morning the old man cut off little dog Turpie's head.

The next night the Hobyahs came again, and said, "Hobyah! Hobyah! Hobyah! Tear down the hempstalks, eat up the old man and woman, and carry off the little girl!" And when the Hobyahs found that little dog Turpie's head was off they tore down the hempstalks, ate up the old man and woman, and carried the little girl off in a bag.

And when the Hobyahs came to their home they hung up the bag with the little girl in it, and every Hobyah knocked on the top of the bag and said, "Look me! look me!" And then they went to sleep until the next night, for the Hobyahs slept in the daytime.

The little girl cried a great deal, and a man with a big dog came that way and heard her crying. When he asked her how she came there and she told him, he put the dog in the bag and took the little girl to his home.

The next night the Hobyahs took down the bag and knocked on the top of it, and said "Look me! look me!" and when they opened the bag—

the big dog jumped out and ate them all up; so there are no Hobyahs now.

A Pottle o' Brains

Once in these parts, and not so long gone neither, there was a fool that wanted to buy a pottle o' brains, for he was ever getting into scrapes through his foolishness, and being laughed at by every one. Folk told him that he could get everything he liked from the wise woman that lived on the top o' the hill, and dealt in potions and herbs and spells and things, and could tell thee! all as 'd come to thee or thy folk. So he told his mother, and asked her if he could seek the wise woman and buy a pottle o' brains.

"That ye should," says she; "thou 'st sore need o' them, my son: and if I should die, who'd take care o' a poor fool such 's thou, no more fit to look after thyself than an unborn baby? but mind thy manners, and speak her pretty, my lad; for they wise folk are gey and light mispleased."

So off he went after his tea, and there she was, sitting by the fire, and stirring a big pot.

"Good e'en, missis," says he, "it's a fine night."

"Aye," says she, and went on stirring.

"It'll maybe rain," says he, and fidgeted from one foot to t' other.

"Maybe," says she.

"And m'appen it won't," says he, and looked out o' the window.

"M'appen," says she.

And he scratched his head and twisted his hat.

"Well," says he, "I can't mind nothing else about the weather, but let me see; the crops are getting on fine."

"Fine," says she.

"And—and—the beasts is fattening," says he.

"They are," says she.

"And—and—" says he, and comes to a stop—"I reckon we'll tackle business now, having done the polite like. Have you any brains for to sell?"

"That depends," says she, "if thou wants king's brains, or soldier's brains, or schoolmaster's brains, I dinna keep 'em."

"Hout no," says he, "jist ordinary brains—fit for any fool—same as every one has about here; something clean common-like."

"Aye so," says the wise woman, "I might manage that, if so be thou 'lt help thyself."

"How's that for, missis?" says he.

"Jest so," says she, looking in the pot; "bring me the heart of the thing thou likest best of all, and I'll tell thee where to get thy pottle o' brains."

"But," says he, scratching his head, "how can I do that?"

"That's no for me to say," says she, "find out for thyself, my lad! if thou doesn't want to be a fool all thy days. But thou 'll have to read me a riddle so as I can see thou 'st brought the right thing, and if thy brains is about thee. And I've something else to see to," says she, "so gode'en to thee," and she carried the pot away with her into the back place.

So off went the fool to his mother, and told her what the wise woman said.

"And I reckon I'll have to kill that pig," says he, "for I like fat bacon better than anything."

"Then do it, my lad," said his mother, "for certain 't will be a strange and good thing fur thee, if thou canst buy a pottle o' brains, and be able to look after thy own self."

So he killed his pig, and next day off he went to the wise woman's cottage, and there she sat, reading in a great book.

"Gode'en, missis," says he, "I've brought thee the heart o' the thing I like the best of all; and I put it hapt in paper on the table."

"Aye so?" says she, and looked at him through her spectacles. "Tell me this then, what runs without feet?"

He scratched his head, and thought, and thought, but he couldn't tell.

"Go thy ways," says she, "thou 'st not fetched me the right thing yet. I've no brains for thee to-day." And she clapt the book together, and turned her back.

So off the fool went to tell his mother. But as he got nigh the house, out came folk running to tell him that his mother was dying.

And when he got in, his mother only looked at him and smiled as if to say she could leave him with a quiet mind since he had got brains enough now to look after himself—and then she died.

So down he sat and the more he thought about it the badder he felt. He minded how she'd nursed him when he was a tiddy brat, and helped him with his lessons, and cooked his dinners, and mended his clouts, and bore with his foolishness; and he felt sorrier and sorrier, while he began to sob and greet.

"Oh, mother, mother!" says he, "who'll take care of me now? Thou shouldn't have left me alone, for I liked thee better than everything!"

And as he said that, he thought of the words of the wise woman. "Hi, yi!" says he, "must I take mother's heart to her?"

"No! I can't do that," says he. "What'll I do? what'll I do to get that pottle o' brains, now I'm alone in the world?" So he thought and thought and thought, and next day he went and borrowed a sack, and bundled his mother in, and carried it on his shoulder up to the wise woman's cottage.

"Gode'en, missis," says he, "I reckon I've fetched thee the right thing this time, surely," and he plumped the sack down kerflap! in the doorsill.

"Maybe," says the wise woman, "but read me this, now, what's yellow and shining but isn't gold?"

And he scratched his head, and thought and thought, but he couldn't tell.

"Thou 'st not hit the right thing, my lad," says she. "I doubt thou 'rt a bigger fool than I thought!" and shut the door in his face.

"See there!" says he, and set down by the road side and greets.

"I've lost the only two things as I cared for, and what else can I find to buy a pottle o' brains with!" and he fair howled, till the tears ran down into his mouth. And up came a lass that lived near at hand, and looked at him.

"What's up with thee, fool?" says she.

"Oo, I've killed my pig, and lost my mother and I'm nobbut a fool myself," says he, sobbing.

"That's bad," says she; "and haven't thee anybody to look after thee?"

"No," says he, "and I canna buy my pottle o' brains, for there's nothing I like best left!"

"What art talking about?" says she.

And down she sets by him, and he told her all about the wise woman and the pig, and his mother and the riddles, and that he was alone in the world.

"Well," says she, "I wouldn't mind looking after thee myself."

"Could thee do it?" says he.

"Ou, ay!" says she; "folks say as fools make good husbands, and I reckon I'll have thee, if thou 'rt willing."

"Can'st cook?" says he.

"Ay, I can," says she.

"And scrub?" says he.

"Surely," says she.

"And mend my clouts?" says he.

"I can that," says she.

"I reckon thou 'lt do then as well as anybody," says he; "but what'll I do about this wise woman?"

"Oh, wait a bit," says she, "something may turn up, and it'll not matter if thou 'rt a fool, so long'st thou 'st got me to look after thee."

"That's true," says he, and off they went and got married. And she kept his house so clean and neat, and cooked his dinner so fine, that one night he says to her: "Lass, I'm thinking I like thee best of everything after all."

"That's good hearing," says she, "and what then?"

"Have I got to kill thee, dost think, and take thy heart up to the wise woman for that pottle o' brains?"

"Law, no!" says she, looking skeered, "I winna have that. But see here; thou didn't cut out thy mother's heart, did thou?"

"No; but if I had, maybe I'd have got my pottle o' brains," says he.

"Not a bit of it," says she; "just thou take me as I be, heart and all, and I'll wager I'll help thee read the riddles."

"Can thee so?" says he, doubtful like; "I reckon they're too hard for women folk."

"Well," says she, "let's see now. Tell me the first"

"What runs without feet?" says he.

"Why, water!" says she.

"It do," says he, and scratched his head.

"And what's yellow and shining but isn't gold?"

"Why, the sun!" says she.

"Faith, it be!" says he. "Come, we'll go up to the wise woman at once," and off they went. And as they came up the pad, she was sitting at the door, twining straws.

"Gode'en, missis," says he.

"Gode'en, fool," says she.

"I reckon I've fetched thee the right thing at last," says he.

The wise woman looked at them both, and wiped her spectacles.

"Canst tell me what that is as has first no legs, and then two legs, and ends with four legs?"

And the fool scratched his head and thought and thought, but he couldn't tell.

And the lass whispered in his ear:

"It's a tadpole."

"M'appen," says he then, "it may be a tadpole, missis."

The wise woman nodded her head.

"That's right," says she, "and thou 'st got thy pottle o' brains already."

"Where be they?" says he, looking about and feeling in his pockets.

"In thy wife's head," says she. "The only cure for a fool is a good wife to look after him, and that thou 'st got, so gode'en to thee!" And with that she nodded to them, and up and into the house.

So they went home together, and he never wanted to buy a pottle o' brains again, for his wife had enough for both.

The King of England and His Three Sons

Once upon a time there was an old king who had three sons; and the old king fell very sick one time and there was nothing at all could make him well but some golden apples from a far country. So the three brothers went on horseback to look for some of these apples. They set off together, and when they came to cross-roads they halted and refreshed themselves a bit; and then they agreed to meet on a certain time, and not one was to go home before the other. So Valentine took the right, and Oliver went straight on, and poor Jack took the left.

To make my long story short, I shall follow poor Jack, and let the other two take their chance, for I don't think there was much good in them. Off poor Jack rides over hills, dales, valleys, and mountains, through woolly woods and sheepwalks, where the old chap never sounded his hollow bugle-horn, farther than I can tell you to-night or ever intend to tell you.

At last he came to an old house, near a great forest, and there was an old man sitting out by the door, and his look was enough to frighten you or any one else; and the old man said to him:

"Good morning, my king's son."

"Good morning to you, old gentleman," was the young prince's answer; frightened out of his wits though he was, he didn't like to give in.

The old gentleman told him to dismount and to go in to have some refreshment, and to put his horse in the stable, such as it was. Jack soon felt much better after having something to eat, and began to ask the old gentleman how he knew he was a king's son.

"Oh dear!" said the old man, "I knew that you were a king's son, and I know what is your business better than what you do yourself. So you will have to stay here to-night; and when you are in bed you mustn't be frightened whatever you may hear. There will come all manner of frogs and snakes, and some will try to get into your eyes and your mouth, but mind, don't stir the least bit or you will turn into one of those things yourself."

Poor Jack didn't know what to make of this, but, however, he ventured to go to bed. Just as he thought to have a bit of sleep, round and over and under him they came, but he never stirred an inch all night.

"Well, my young son, how are you this morning?"

"Oh, I am very well, thank you, but I didn't have much rest."

"Well, never mind that; you have got on very well so far, but you have a great deal to go through before you can have the golden apples to go to your father. You'd better come and have some breakfast before you start on your way to my other brother's house. You will have to leave your own horse here with me until you come back again, and tell me everything about how you get on."

After that out came a fresh horse for the young prince, and the old man gave him a ball of yarn, and he flung it between the horse's two ears.

Off he went as fast as the wind, which the wind behind could not catch the wind before, until he came to the second oldest brother's house. When he rode up to the door he had the same salute as from the first old man, but this one was even uglier than the first one. He had long grey hair, and his teeth were curling out of his mouth, and his finger- and toe-nails had not been cut for many thousand years. He put the horse into a much better stable, and called Jack in, and gave him plenty to eat and drink, and they had a bit of a chat before they went to bed.

"Well, my young son," said the old man, "I suppose you are one of the king's children come to look for the golden apples to bring him back to health."

"Yes, I am the youngest of the three brothers, and I should like to get them to go back with."

"Well, don't mind, my young son. Before you go to bed to-night I will send to my eldest brother, and will tell him what you want, and he won't have much trouble in sending you on to the place where you must get the apples. But mind not to stir to-night no matter how you get bitten and stung, or else you will work great mischief to yourself."

The young man went to bed and bore all, as he did the first night, and got up the next morning well and hearty. After a good breakfast out comes a fresh horse, and a ball of yarn to throw between his ears. The old man told him to jump up quick, and said that he had made it all right with his eldest brother, not to delay for anything whatever, "For," said he, "you have a good deal to go through with in a very short and quick time."

He flung the ball, and off he goes as quick as lightning, and comes to the eldest brother's house. The old man receives him very kindly and told him he long wished to see him, and that he would go through his work like a man and come back safe and sound. "To-night," said he, "I will give you rest; there shall nothing come to disturb you, so that you may not feel sleepy for to-morrow. And you must mind to get up middling early, for you've got to go and come all in the same day; there will be no place for you to rest within thousands of miles of that place; and if there was, you would stand in great danger never to come from there in your own form. Now, my young prince, mind what I tell you. To-morrow, when you come in sight of a very large castle, which will be surrounded with black water, the first thing you will do you will tie your horse to a tree, and you will see three beautiful swans in sight, and you will say, 'Swan, swan, carry me over in the name of the Griffin of the Greenwood,' and the swans will swim you over to the earth. There will be three great entrances, the first guarded by four great giants with drawn swords in their hands, the second by lions, the other by fiery serpents and dragons. You will have to be there exactly at one o'clock; and mind and leave there precisely at two and not a moment later. When the swans carry you over to the castle, you will pass all these things, all fast asleep, but you must not notice any of them.

"When you go in, you will turn up to the right; you will see some grand rooms, then you will go downstairs through the cooking kitchen, and through; a door on your left you go into a garden, where you will find the apples you want for your father to get well. After you fill your wallet, you make all speed you possibly can, and call out for the swans to carry you over the same as before. After you get on your horse, should you hear anything shouting or making any noise after you, be sure not to look back, as they will follow you for thousands of miles; but when the time is up and you get near my place, it will be all over. Well now, my young man, I have told you all you have to do to-morrow; and mind, whatever you do, don't look about you when you see all those frightful things asleep. Keep a good heart, and make haste from there, and come back to me with all the speed you can. I should like to know how my two brothers were when you left them, and what they said to you about me."

**The Castle of Melvales
Swan Swan, Carry me over, In the name
of the Griffin of Greenwood.**

"Well, to tell the truth, before I left London my father was sick, and said I was to come here to look for the golden apples, for they were the only things that would do him good; and when I came to your youngest brother, he told me many things I had to do before I came here. And I thought once that your youngest brother put me in the wrong bed, when he put all those snakes to bite me all night long, until your second brother told me 'So it was to be,' and said, 'It is the same here,' but said you had none in your beds."

"Well, let's go to bed. You need not fear. There are no snakes here."

The young man went to bed, and had a good night's rest, and got up the next morning as fresh as newly caught trout. Breakfast being over, out comes the other horse, and, while saddling and fettling, the old man began to laugh, and told the young gentleman that if he saw a pretty young lady, not to stay with her too long, because she might waken, and then he would have to stay with her or to be turned into one of those unearthly monsters, like those he would have to pass by going into the castle.

"Ha! ha! ha! you make me laugh so that I can scarcely buckle the saddle-straps. I think I shall make it all right, my uncle, if I see a young lady there, you may depend."

"Well, my boy, I shall see how you will get on."

So he mounts his Arab steed, and off he goes like a shot out of a gun. At last he comes in sight of the castle. He ties his horse safe to a tree, and pulls out his watch. It was then a quarter to one, when he called out, "Swan, swan, carry me over, for the name of the old Griffin of the Greenwood." No sooner said than done. A swan under each side, and one in front, took him over in a crack. He got on his legs, and walked quietly by all those giants, lions, fiery serpents, and all manner of other frightful things too numerous to mention, while they were fast asleep, and that only for the space of one hour, when into the castle he goes neck or nothing. Turning to the right, upstairs he runs, and enters into a very grand bedroom, and sees a beautiful Princess lying full stretch on a gold bedstead, fast asleep. He gazed on her beautiful form with admiration, and he takes her garter off, and buckles it on his own leg, and he buckles his on hers; he also takes her gold watch and pocket-handkerchief, and exchanges his for hers; after that he ventures to give her a kiss, when she very nearly opened her eyes. Seeing the time short, off he runs downstairs, and passing through the kitchen to go into the garden for the apples, he could see the cook all-fours on her back on the middle of the floor, with the knife in one hand and the fork in the other. He found the apples, and filled the wallet; and on passing through the kitchen the cook near wakened, but he was obliged to make all the speed he possibly could, as the time was nearly up. He called out for the swans, and they managed to take him over; but they found that he was a little heavier than before. No sooner than he had mounted his horse he could hear a tremendous noise, the enchantment was broke, and they tried to follow him, but all to no purpose. He was not long before he came to the oldest brother's house; and glad enough he was to see it, for the sight and the noise of all those things that were after him nearly frightened him to death.

"Welcome, my boy; I am proud to see you. Dismount and put the horse in the stable, and come in and have some refreshments; I know you are hungry after all you have gone through in that castle. And tell me all you did, and all you saw there. Other kings' sons went by here to go to that castle, but they never came back alive, and you are the only one that ever broke the spell. And now you must come with me, with a sword in your hand, and must cut my head off, and must throw it in that well."

The young Prince dismounts, and puts his horse in the stable, and they go in to have some refreshments, for I can assure you he wanted some; and after telling everything that passed, which the old gentleman was very pleased to hear, they both went for a walk together, the young Prince looking around and seeing the place looking dreadful, as did the old man. He could scarcely walk from his toe-nails curling up like ram's horns that had not been cut for many hundred years, and big long hair. They come to a well, and the old man gives the Prince a sword, and tells him to cut his head off, and throw it in that well. The young man has to do it against his wish, but has to do it.

No sooner has he flung the head in the well, than up springs one of the finest young gentlemen you would wish to see; and instead of the old house and the frightful-looking place, it was changed into a beautiful hall and grounds. And they went back and enjoyed themselves well, and had a good laugh about the castle.

The young Prince leaves this young gentleman in all his glory, and he tells the young Prince before leaving that he will see him again before long. They have a jolly shake-hands, and off he goes to the next oldest brother; and, to make my long story short, he has to serve the other two brothers the same as the first.

Now the youngest brother began to ask him how things went on. "Did you see my two brothers?"

"Yes."

"How did they look?"

"Oh! they looked very well. I liked them much. They told me many things what to do."

"Well, did you go to the castle?"

"Yes, my uncle."

"And will you tell me what you see in there? Did you see the young lady?"

"Yes, I saw her, and plenty of other frightful things."

"Did you hear any snake biting you in my oldest brother's bed?"

"No, there were none there; I slept well."

"You won't have to sleep in the same bed to-night. You will have to cut my head off in the morning."

The young Prince had a good night's rest, and changed all the appearance of the place by cutting his friend's head off before he started in the morning. A jolly shake-hands, and the uncle tells him it's very probable he shall see him again soon when he is not aware of it. This one's mansion was very pretty, and the country around it beautiful, after his head was cut off. Off Jack goes, over hills, dales, valleys, and mountains, and very near losing his apples again.

At last he arrives at the cross-roads, where he has to meet his brothers on the very day appointed. Coming up to the place, he sees no tracks of horses, and, being very tired, he lays himself down to sleep, by tying the horse to his leg, and putting the apples under his head. Presently up come the other brothers the same time to the minute, and found him fast asleep; and they would not waken him, but said one to another, "Let us see what sort of apples he has got under his head." So they took and tasted them, and found they were different to theirs. They took and changed his apples for theirs, and off to London as fast as they could, and left the poor fellow sleeping.

After a while he awoke, and, seeing the tracks of other horses, he mounted and off with him, not thinking anything about the apples being changed. He had still a long way to go, and by the time he got near London he could hear all the bells in the town ringing, but did not know what was the matter till he rode up to the palace, when he came to know that his father was recovered by his brothers' apples. When he got there his two brothers were off to some sports for a while; and the King was glad to see his youngest son, and very anxious to taste his apples. But when he found out that they were not good, and thought that they were more for poisoning him, he sent immediately for the headsman to behead his youngest son, who was taken away there and then in a carriage. But instead of the headsman taking his head off, he took him to a forest not far from the town, because he had pity on him, and there left him to take his chance, when presently up comes a big hairy bear, limping upon three legs. The Prince, poor fellow, climbed up a tree, frightened of him, but the bear told him to come down, that it was no use of him to stop there. With hard persuasion poor Jack comes down, and the bear speaks to him and bids him "Come here to me; I will not do you any harm. It's better for you to come with me and have some refreshments; I know that you are hungry all this time."

The poor young Prince says, "No, I am not hungry; but I was very frightened when I saw you coming to me first, as I had no place to run away from you."

The bear said, "I was also afraid of you when I saw that gentleman setting you down from the carriage. I thought you would have guns with you, and that you would not mind killing me if you saw me; but when I saw the gentleman going away with the carriage, and leaving you behind by yourself, I made bold to come to you, to see who you were, and now I know who you are very well. Are you not the king's youngest son? I have seen you and your brothers and lots of other gentlemen in this wood many times. Now before we go from here, I must tell you that I am in disguise; and I shall take you where we are stopping."

The young Prince tells him everything from first to last, how he started in search of the apples, and about the three old men, and about the castle, and how he was served at last by his father after he came home; and instead of the headsman taking his head off, he was kind enough to leave him his life, "and here I am now, under your protection."

The bear tells him, "Come on, my brother; there shall no harm come to you as long as you are with me."

So he takes him up to the tents; and when they see 'em coming, the girls begin to laugh, and say, "Here is our Jubal coming with a young gentleman." When he advanced nearer the tents, they all knew that he was the young Prince that had passed by that way many times before; and when Jubal went to change himself, he called most of them together into one tent, and told them all about him, and to be kind to him. And so they were, for there was nothing that he desired but what he had, the same as if he was in the palace with his father and mother. Jubal, after he pulled off his hairy coat, was one of the finest young men amongst them, and he was the young Prince's closest companion. The young Prince was always very sociable and merry, only when he thought of the gold watch he had from the young Princess in the castle, and which he had lost he knew not where.

He passed off many happy days in the forest; but one day he and poor Jubal were strolling through the trees, when they came to the very spot where they first met, and, accidentally looking up, he could see his watch hanging in the tree which he had to climb when he first saw poor Jubal coming to him in the form of a bear; and he cries out, "Jubal, Jubal, I can see my watch up in that tree."

"Well, I am sure, how lucky!" exclaimed poor Jubal; "shall I go and get it down?"

"No, I'd rather go myself," said the young Prince.

Now whilst all this was going on, the young Princess in that castle, seeing that one of the King of England's sons had been there by the changing of the watch and other things, got herself ready with a large army, and sailed off for England. She left her army a little out of the town, and she went with her guards straight up to the palace to see the King, and also demanded to see his sons. They had a long conversation together about different things. At last she demands one of the sons to come before her; and the oldest comes, when she asks him, "Have you ever been at the Castle of Melvales?" and he answers, "Yes." She throws down a pocket handkerchief and bids him to walk over it without stumbling. He goes to walk over it, and no sooner did he put his foot on it, than he fell down and broke his leg. He was taken off immediately and made a prisoner of by her own guards. The other was called upon, and was asked the same questions, and I had to go through the same performance, and he also was made a prisoner of. Now she says, "Have you not another son?" when the King began so to shiver and shake and knock his two knees together that he could scarcely stand upon his legs, and did not know what to say to her, he was so much frightened. At last a thought came to him to send for his headsman, and inquire of him particularly, Did he behead his son, or was he alive?

"He is saved, O King."

"Then bring him here immediately, or else I shall be done for."

Two of the fastest horses they had were put in the carriage, to go and look for the poor Prince; and when they got to the very spot where they left him, it was the time when the Prince was up the tree, getting his watch down, and poor Jubal standing a distance off. They cried out to him, Had he seen another young man in this wood? Jubal, seeing such a nice carriage, thought something, and did not like to say No, and said Yes, and pointed up the tree; and they told him to come down immediately, as there was a young lady in search of him.

"Ha! ha! ha! Jubal, did you ever hear such a thing in all your life, my brother?"

"Do you call him your brother?"

"Well, he has been better to me than my brothers."

"Well, for his kindness he shall accompany you to the palace, and see how things turn out."

After they go to the palace, the Prince has a good wash, and appears before the Princess, when she asks him, Had he ever been at the Castle of Melvales? With a smile upon his face, he gives a graceful bow. And says my Lady, "Walk over that handkerchief without stumbling." He walks over it many times, and dances upon it, and nothing happened to him. She said, with a proud and smiling air, "That is the young man;" and out come the objects exchanged by both of them. Presently she orders a very large box to be brought in and to be opened, and out come some of the most costly uniforms that were ever worn on an emperor's back; and when he dressed himself up, the King could scarcely look upon him from the dazzling of the gold and diamonds on his coat. He orders his two brothers to be in confinement for a period of time; and before the Princess asks him to go with her to her own country, she pays a visit to the bear's camp, and she makes some very handsome presents for their kindness to the young Prince. And she gives Jubal an invitation to go with them, which he accepts; wishes them a hearty farewell for a while, promising to see them all again in some little time.

They go back to the King and bid farewell, and tell him not to be so hasty another time to order people to be beheaded before having a proper cause for it. Off they go with all their army with them; but while the soldiers were striking their tents, the Prince bethought himself of his Welsh harp, and had it sent for immediately to take with him in a beautiful wooden case. They called to see each of those three brothers whom the Prince had to stay with when he was on his way to the Castle of Melvales; and I can assure you, when they all got together, they had a very merry time of it. And there we will leave them.

King John and the Abbot of Canterbury

In the reign of King John there lived an Abbot of Canterbury who kept up grand state in his Abbey. A hundred of the Abbot's men dined each day with him in his refectory, and fifty knights in velvet coats and gold chains waited upon him daily. Well, King John, as you know, was a very bad king, and he couldn't brook the idea of any one in his kingdom, however holy he might be, being honoured more than he. So he summoned the Abbot of Canterbury to his presence.

The Abbot came with a goodly retinue, with his fifty knights-at-arms in velvet cloaks and gold chains. The King went to meet him, and said to him, "How now, father Abbot? I hear it of thee, thou keepest far greater state than I. This becomes not our royal dignity, and savours of treason in thee."

"My liege," quoth the Abbot, bending low, "I beg to say that all I spend has been freely given to the Abbey out of the piety of the folk. I trust your Grace will not take it ill that I spend for the Abbey's sake what is the Abbey's."

"Nay, proud prelate," answered the King, "all that is in this fair realm of England is our own, and thou hast no right to put me to shame by holding such state. However, of my clemency I will spare thee thy life and thy property if you can answer me but three questions."

"I will do so, my liege," said the Abbot, "so far as my poor wit can extend."

"Well, then," said the King, "tell me where is the centre of all the world round; then let me know how soon can I ride the whole world about; and, lastly, tell me what I think."

"Your Majesty jesteth," stammered the Abbot.

"Thou wilt find it no jest," said the King. "Unless thou canst answer me these questions three before a week is out, thy head will leave thy body;" and he turned away.

Well, the Abbot rode off in fear and trembling, and first he went to Oxford to see if any learned doctor could tell him the answer to those questions three; but none could help him, and he took his way to Canterbury, sad and sorrowful, to take leave of his monks. But on his way he met his shepherd as he was going to the fold.

"Welcome home, Lord Abbot," quoth the shepherd; "what news from good King John?"

"Sad news, sad news, my shepherd," said the Abbot, and told him all that had happened.

"Now, cheer up, Sir Abbot," said the shepherd. "A fool may perhaps answer what a wise man knows not. I will go to London in your stead; grant me only your apparel and your retinue of knights. At the least I can die in your place."

"Nay, shepherd, not so," said the Abbot; "I must meet the danger in my own person. And to that, thou canst not pass for me."

"But I can and I will, Sir Abbot. In a cowl, who will know me for what I am?"

So at last the Abbot consented, and sent him to London in his most splendid array, and he approached King John with all his retinue as before, but dressed in his simple monk's dress and his cowl over his face.

"Now welcome, Sir Abbot," said King John; "thou art prepared for thy doom, I see."

"I am ready to answer your Majesty," said he.

"Well, then, question first—where is the centre of the round earth?" said the King.

"Here," said the shepherd Abbot, planting his crozier in the ground; "an' your Majesty believe me not, go measure it and see."

"By St. Botolph," said the King, "a merry answer and a shrewd; so to question the second. How soon may I ride this round world about?"

"If your Majesty will graciously rise with the sun, and ride along with him until the next morning he rise, your Grace will surely have ridden it round."

"By St. John," laughed King John, "I did not think it could be done so soon. But let that pass, and tell me question third and last, and that is—What do I think?"

"That is easy, your Grace," said he. "Your Majesty thinks I am my lord the Abbot of Canterbury; but as you may see," and here he raised his cowl, "I am but his poor shepherd, that am come to ask your pardon for him and for me."

Loud laughed the King. "Well caught. Thou hast more wit than thy lord, and thou shalt be Abbot in his place."

"Nay, that cannot be," quoth the shepherd; "I know not to write nor to read."

"Well, then, four nobles a week thou shalt have for the ready wit. And tell the Abbot from me that he has my pardon." And with that King John sent away the shepherd with a right royal present, besides his pension.

Rushen Coatie

There was once a king and a queen, as many a one has been; few have we seen, and as few may we see. But the queen died, leaving only one bonny girl, and she told her on her death-bed: "My dear, after I am gone, there will come to you a little red calf, and whenever you want anything, speak to it, and it will give it you."

Now, after a while, the king married again an ill-natured wife, with three ugly daughters of her own. And they hated the king's daughter because she was so bonny. So they took all her fine clothes away from her, and gave her only a coat made of rushes. So they called her Rushen Coatie, and made her sit in the kitchen nook, amid the ashes. And when dinner-time came, the nasty stepmother sent her out a thimbleful of broth, a grain of barley, a thread of meat, and a crumb of bread. But when she had eaten all this, she was just as hungry as before, so she said to herself: "Oh! how I wish I had something to eat." Just then, who should come in but a little red calf, and said to her: "Put your finger into my left ear." She did so, and found some nice bread. Then the calf told her to put her finger into its right ear, and she found there some cheese, and made a right good meal of the bread and cheese. And so it went on from day to day.

Now the king's wife thought Rushen Coatie would soon die from the scanty food she got, and she was surprised to see her as lively and healthy as ever. So she set one of her ugly daughters on the watch at meal times to find out how Rushen Coatie got enough to live on. The daughter soon found out that the red calf gave food to Rushen Coatie, and told her mother. So her mother went to the king and told him she was longing to have a sweetbread from a red calf. Then the king sent for his butcher, and had the little red calf killed. And when Rushen Coatie heard of it, she sate down and wept by its side, but the dead calf said:

"Take me up, bone by bone,
And put me beneath yon grey stone;
When there is aught you want
Tell it me, and that I'll grant."

So she did so, but could not find the shank-bone of the calf.

Now the very next Sunday was Yuletide, and all the folk were going to church in their best clothes, so Rushen Coatie said: "Oh! I should like to go to church, too," but the three ugly sisters said: "What would you do at the church, you nasty thing? You must bide at home and make the dinner." And the king's wife said: "And this is what you must make the soup of, a thimbleful of water, a grain of barley, and a crumb of bread."

When they all went to church, Rushen Coatie sat down and wept, but looking up, who should she see coming in limping, lamping, with a shank wanting, but the dear red calf? And the red calf said to her: "Do not sit there weeping, but go, put on these clothes, and above all, put on this pair of glass slippers, and go your way to church."

"But what will become of the dinner?" said Rushen Coatie.

"Oh, do not fash about that," said the red calf, "all you have to do is to say to the fire:

"'Every peat make t'other burn,
Every spit make t'other turn,
Every pot make t'other play,
Till I come from church this good Yuleday,'

and be off to church with you. But mind you come home first."

So Rushen Coatie said this, and went off to church, and she was the grandest and finest lady there. There happened to be a young prince there, and he fell at once in love with her. But she came away before service was over, and was home before the rest, and had off her fine clothes and on with her rushen coatie, and she found the calf had covered the table, and the dinner was ready, and everything was in good order when the rest came home. The three sisters said to Rushen Coatie: "Eh, lassie, if you had seen the bonny fine lady in church to-day, that the young prince fell in love with!" Then she said: "Oh! I wish you would let me go with you to the church to-morrow," for they used to go three days together to church at Yuletide.

But they said: "What should the like of you do at church, nasty thing? The kitchen nook is good enough for you."

So the next day they all went to church, and Rushen Coatie was left behind, to make dinner out of a thimbleful of water, a grain of barley, a crumb of bread, and a thread of meat. But the red calf came to her help again, gave her finer clothes than before, and she went to church, where all the world was looking at her, and wondering where such a grand lady came from, and the prince fell more in love with her than ever, and tried to find out where she went to. But she was too quick for him, and got home long before the rest, and the red calf had the dinner all ready.

The next day the calf dressed her in even grander clothes than before, and she went to the church. And the young prince was there again, and this time he put a guard at the door to keep her, but she took a hop and a run and jumped over their heads, and as she did so, down fell one of her glass slippers. She didn't wait to pick it up, you may be sure, but off she ran home, as fast as she could go, on with the rushen coatie, and the calf had all things ready.

Then the young prince put out a proclamation that whoever could put on the glass slipper should be his bride. All the ladies of his court went and tried to put on the slipper. And they tried and tried and tried, but it was too small for them all. Then he ordered one of his ambassadors to mount a fleet horse and ride through the kingdom and find an owner for the glass shoe. He rode and he rode to town and castle, and made all the ladies try to put on the shoe. Many a one tried to get it on that she might be the prince's bride. But no, it wouldn't do, and many a one wept, I warrant, because she couldn't get on the bonny glass shoe. The ambassador rode on and on till he came at the very last to the house where there were the three ugly sisters. The first two tried it and it wouldn't do, and the queen, mad with spite, hacked off the toes and heels of the third sister, and she could then put the slipper on, and the prince was brought to marry her, for he had to keep his promise. The ugly sister was dressed all in her best and was put up behind the prince on horseback, and off they rode in great gallantry. But ye all know, pride must have a fall, for as they rode along a raven sang out of a bush—

"Hackèd Heels and Pinchèd Toes
Behind the young prince rides,
But Pretty Feet and Little Feet
Behind the cauldron bides."

"What's that the birdie sings?" said the young prince.

"Nasty, lying thing," said the step-sister, "never mind what it says."

But the prince looked down and saw the slipper dripping with blood, so he rode back and put her down. Then he said, "There must be some one that the slipper has not been tried on."

"Oh, no," said they, "there's none but a dirty thing that sits in the kitchen nook and wears a rushen coatie."

But the prince was determined to try it on Rushen Coatie, but she ran away to the grey stone, where the red calf dressed her in her bravest dress, and she went to the prince and the slipper jumped out of his pocket on to her foot, fitting her without any chipping or paring. So the prince married her that very day, and they lived happy ever after.

The King o' the Cats

One winter's evening the sexton's wife was sitting by the fireside with her big black cat, Old Tom, on the other side, both half asleep and waiting for the master to come home. They waited and they waited, but still he didn't come, till at last he came rushing in, calling out, "Who's Tommy Tildrum?" in such a wild way that both his wife and his cat stared at him to know what was the matter.

"Why, what's the matter?" said his wife, "and why do you want to know who Tommy Tildrum is?"

"Oh, I've had such an adventure. I was digging away at old Mr. Fordyce's grave when I suppose I must have dropped asleep, and only woke up by hearing a cat's *Miaou*."

"*Miaou!*" said Old Tom in answer.

"Yes, just like that! So I looked over the edge of the grave, and what do you think I saw?"

"Now, how can I tell?" said the sexton's wife.

"Why, nine black cats all like our friend Tom here, all with a white spot on their chestesses. And what do you think they were carrying? Why, a small coffin covered with a black velvet pall, and on the pall was a small coronet all of gold, and at every third step they took they cried all together, *Miaou*—"

"*Miaou!*" said Old Tom again.

"Yes, just like that!" said the Sexton; "and as they came nearer and nearer to me I could see them more distinctly, because their eyes shone out with a sort of green light. Well, they all came towards me, eight of them carrying the coffin, and the biggest cat of all walking in front for all the world like—but look at our Tom, how he's looking at me. You'd think he knew all I was saying."

"Go on, go on," said his wife; "never mind Old Tom."

"Well, as I was a-saying, they came towards me slowly and solemnly, and at every third step crying all together, *Miaou!*—"

"*Miaou!*" said Old Tom again.

"Yes, just like that, till they came and stood right opposite Mr. Fordyce's grave, where I was, when they all stood still and looked straight at me. I did feel queer, that I did! But look at Old Tom; he's looking at me just like they did."

"Go on, go on," said his wife; "never mind Old Tom."

"Where was I? Oh, they all stood still looking at me, when the one that wasn't carrying the coffin came forward and, staring straight at me, said to me—yes, I tell 'ee, *said* to me, with a squeaky voice, 'Tell Tom Tildrum that Tim Toldrum's dead,' and that's why I asked you if you knew who Tom Tildrum was, for how can I tell Tom Tildrum Tim Toldrum's dead if I don't know who Tom Tildrum is?"

"Look at Old Tom, look at Old Tom!" screamed his wife.

And well he might look, for Tom was swelling and Tom was staring, and at last Tom shrieked out, "What—old Tim dead! then I'm the King o' the Cats!" and rushed up the chimney and was never more seen.

Tamlane

Young Tamlane was son of Earl Murray, and Burd Janet was daughter of Dunbar, Earl of March. And when they were young they loved one another and plighted their troth. But when the time came near for their marrying, Tamlane disappeared, and none knew what had become of him.

Many, many days after he had disappeared, Burd Janet was wandering in Carterhaugh Wood, though she had been warned not to go there. And as she wandered she plucked the flowers from the bushes. She came at last to a bush of broom and began plucking it. She had not taken more than three flowerets when by her side up started young Tamlane.

"Where come ye from, Tamlane, Tamlane?" Burd Janet said; "and why have you been away so long?"

"From Elfland I come," said young Tamlane. "The Queen of Elfland has made me her knight."

"But how did you get there, Tamlane?" said Burd Janet.

"I was hunting one day, and as I rode widershins round yon hill, a deep drowsiness fell upon me, and when I awoke, behold! I was in Elfland. Fair is that land and gay, and fain would I stop but for thee and one other thing. Every seven years the Elves pay their tithe to the Nether world, and for all the Queen makes much of me, I fear it is myself that will be the tithe."

"Oh can you not be saved? Tell me if aught I can do will save you, Tamlane?"

"One only thing is there for my safety. To-morrow night is Hallowe'en, and the fairy court will then ride through England and Scotland, and if you would borrow me from Elfland you must take your stand by Miles Cross between twelve and one o' the night, and with holy water in your hand you must cast a compass all around you."

"But how shall I know you, Tamlane?" quoth Burd Janet, "amid so many knights I've ne'er seen before?"

"The first court of Elves that come by let pass. The next court you shall pay reverence to, but do naught nor say aught. But the third court that comes by is the chief court of them, and at the head rides the Queen of all Elfland. And I shall ride by her side upon a milk-white steed with a star in my crown; they give me this honour as being a christened knight. Watch my hands, Janet, the right one will be gloved but the left one will be bare, and by that token you will know me."

"But how to save you, Tamlane?" quoth Burd Janet.

"You must spring upon me suddenly, and I will fall to the ground. Then seize me quick, and whatever change befall me, for they will exercise all their magic on me, cling hold to me till they turn me into red-hot iron. Then cast me into this pool and I will be turned back into a mother-naked man. Cast then your green mantle over me, and I shall be yours, and be of the world again."

So Burd Janet promised to do all for Tamlane, and next night at midnight she took her stand by Miles Cross and cast a compass round her with holy water.

Soon there came riding by the Elfin court, first over the mound went a troop on black steeds, and then another troop on brown. But in the third court, all on milk-white steeds, she saw the Queen of Elfland, and by her side a knight with a star in his crown, with right hand gloved and the left bare. Then she knew this was her own Tamlane, and springing forward she seized the bridle of the milk-white steed and pulled its rider down. And as soon as he had touched the ground she let go the bridle and seized him in her arms.

"He's won, he's won amongst us all," shrieked out the eldritch crew, and all came around her and tried their spells on young Tamlane.

First they turned him in Janet's arms like frozen ice, then into a huge flame of roaring fire. Then, again, the fire vanished and an adder was skipping through her arms, but still she held on; and then they turned him into a snake that reared up as if to bite her, and yet she held on. Then suddenly a dove was struggling in her arms, and almost flew away. Then they turned him into a swan, but all was in vain, till at last he was turned into a red-hot glaive, and this she cast into a well of water and then he turned back into a mother-naked man. She quickly cast her green mantle over him, and young Tamlane was Burd Janet's for ever.

Then sang the Queen of Elfland as the court turned away and began to resume its march:

"She that has borrowed young Tamlane
Has gotten a stately groom,
She's taken away my bonniest knight,
Left nothing in his room.

"But had I known, Tamlane, Tamlane,
A lady would borrow thee,
I'd hae ta'en out thy two grey eyne,
Put in two eyne of tree.

"Had I but known, Tamlane, Tamlane,
Before we came from home,
I'd hae ta'en out thy heart o' flesh,
Put in a heart of stone.

"Had I but had the wit yestreen
That I have got to-day,
I'd paid the Fiend seven times his teind
Ere you'd been won away."

And then the Elfin court rode away, and Burd Janet and young Tamlane went their way homewards and were soon after married after young Tamlane had again been sained by the holy water and made Christian once more.

The Stars in the Sky

Once on a time and twice on a time, and all times together as ever I heard tell of, there was a tiny lassie who would weep all day to have the stars in the sky to play with; she wouldn't have this, and she wouldn't have that, but it was always the stars she would have. So one fine day off she went to find them. And she walked and she walked and she walked, till by-and-by she came to a mill-dam.

"Goode'en to ye," says she, "I'm seeking the stars in the sky to play with. Have you seen any?"

"Oh, yes, my bonnie lassie," said the mill-dam. "They shine in my own face o' nights till I can't sleep for them. Jump in and perhaps you'll find one."

So she jumped in, and swam about and swam about and swam about, but ne'er a one could she see. So she went on till she came to a brooklet.

"Goode'en to ye, Brooklet, Brooklet," says she; "I'm seeking the stars in the sky to play with. Have you seen any?"

"Yes, indeed, my bonny lassie," said the Brooklet. "They glint on my banks at night. Paddle about, and maybe you'll find one."

So she paddled and she paddled and she paddled, but ne'er a one did she find. So on she went till she came to the Good Folk.

"Goode'en to ye, Good Folk," says she; "I'm looking for the stars in the sky to play with. Have ye seen e'er a one?"

"Why, yes, my bonny lassie," said the Good Folk. "They shine on the grass here o' night. Dance with us, and maybe you'll find one."

And she danced and she danced and she danced, but ne'er a one did she see. So down she sate; I suppose she wept.

"Oh dearie me, oh dearie me," says she, "I've swam and I've paddled and I've danced, and if ye'll not help me I shall never find the stars in the sky to play with."

But the Good Folk whispered together, and one of them came up to her and took her by the hand and said, "If you won't go home to your mother, go forward, go forward; mind you take the right road. Ask Four Feet to carry you to No Feet at all, and tell No Feet at all to carry you to the stairs without steps, and if you can climb that—"

"Oh, shall I be among the stars in the sky then?" cried the lassie.

"If you'll not be, then you'll be elsewhere," said the Good Folk, and set to dancing again.

So on she went again with a light heart, and by-and-by she came to a saddled horse, tied to a tree.

"Goode'en to ye, Beast," said she; "I'm seeking the stars in the sky to play with. Will you give me a lift, for all my bones are an-aching."

"Nay," said the horse, "I know nought of the stars in the sky, and I'm here to do the bidding of the Good Folk, and not my own will."

"Well," said she, "it's from the Good Folk I come, and they bade me tell Four Feet to carry me to No Feet at all."

"That's another story," said he; "jump up and ride with me."

So they rode and they rode and they rode, till they got out of the forest and found themselves at the edge of the sea. And on the water in front of them was a wide glistening path running straight out towards a beautiful thing that rose out of the water and went up into the sky, and was all the colours in the world, blue and red and green, and wonderful to look at.

"Now get you down," said the horse; "I've brought ye to the end of the land, and that's as much as Four Feet can do. I must away home to my own folk."

"But," said the lassie, "where's No Feet at all, and where's the stair without steps?"

"I know not," said the horse, "it's none of my business neither. So goode'en to ye, my bonny lassie;" and off he went.

So the lassie stood still and looked at the water, till a strange kind of fish came swimming up to her feet.

"Goode'en to ye, big Fish," says she, "I'm looking for the stars in the sky, and for the stairs that climb up to them. Will ye show me the way?"

"Nay," said the Fish, "I can't unless you bring me word from the Good Folk."

"Yes, indeed," said she. "They said Four Feet would bring me to No Feet at all, and No Feet at all would carry me to the stairs without steps."

"Ah, well," said the Fish; "that's all right then. Get on my back and hold fast."

And off he went—Kerplash!—into the water, along the silver path, towards the bright arch. And the nearer they came the brighter the sheen of it, till she had to shade her eyes from the light of it.

And as they came to the foot of it, she saw it was a broad bright road, sloping up and away into the sky, and at the far, far end of it she could see wee shining things dancing about.

"Now," said the Fish, "here you are, and yon's the stair; climb up, if you can, but hold on fast. I'll warrant you find the stair easier at home than by such a way; 't was ne'er meant for lassies' feet to travel;" and off he splashed through the water.

So she clomb and she clomb and she clomb, but ne'er a step higher did she get: the light was before her and around her, and the water behind her, and the more she struggled the more she was forced down into the dark and the cold, and the more she clomb the deeper she fell.

But she clomb and she clomb, till she got dizzy in the light and shivered with the cold, and dazed with the fear; but still she clomb, till at last, quite dazed and silly-like, she let clean go, and sank down—down—down.

And bang she came on to the hard boards, and found herself sitting, weeping and wailing, by the bedside at home all alone.

News!

MR. G. Ha! Steward, how are you, my old boy? How do things go on at home?

STEWARD. Bad enough, your honour; the magpie's dead!

MR. G. Poor mag! so he's gone. How came he to die?

STEWARD. Over-ate himself, Sir.

MR. G. Did he indeed? a greedy dog. Why, what did he get that he liked so well?

STEWARD. Horseflesh; he died of eating horseflesh.

MR. G. How came he to get so much horseflesh?

STEWARD. All your father's horses, Sir.

MR. G. What! are they dead too?

STEWARD. Ay, Sir; they died of over-work.

MR. G. And why were they over-worked?

STEWARD. To carry water, Sir.

MR. G. To carry water, and what were they carrying water for?

STEWARD. Sure, Sir, to put out the fire.

MR. G. Fire! what fire?

STEWARD. Your father's house is burned down to the ground.

MR. G. My father's house burnt down! and how came it to be on fire?

STEWARD. I think, Sir, it must have been the torches.

MR G. Torches! what torches?

STEWARD. At your mother's funeral.

MR. G. My mother dead?

STEWARD. Ay, poor lady, she never looked up after it.

MR. G. After what?

STEWARD. The loss of your father.

MR. G. My father gone too?

STEWARD. Yes, poor gentleman, he took to his bed as soon as he heard of it.

MR. G. Heard of what?

STEWARD. The bad news, an' it please your honour.

MR. G. What? more miseries, more bad news!

STEWARD. Yes, Sir, your bank has failed, your credit is lost and you're not worth a shilling in the world. I make bold, Sir, to come and wait on you about it; for I thought you would like to hear the news.

Puddock, Mousie, and Ratton

There lived a Puddock in a well,
And a merry Mousie in a mill.

Puddock he would a-wooing rid
Sword and pistol by his side.

Puddock came to the Mousie's inn,
"Mistress Mousie, are you within?"

MOUSIE.

"Yes, kind Sir, I am within,
Softly do I sit and spin."

PUDDOCK.

"Madam, I am come to woo,
Marriage I must have of you."

MOUSIE.

"Marriage I will grant you none
Till Uncle Ratton he comes home."

PUDDOCK.

"See, Uncle Ratton's now come in
Then go and bask the bride within."

Who is it that sits next the wall

But Lady Mousie both slim and small?

Who is it that sits next the bride
But Lord Puddock with yellow side?

But soon came Duckie and with her Sir Drake;
Duckie takes Puddock and makes him squeak.

Then came in the old carl cat
With a fiddle on his back:
"Do ye any music lack?"

Puddock he swam down the brook,
Sir Drake he catched him in his fluke.

The cat he pulled Lord Ratton down,
The kittens they did claw his crown.

But Lady Mousie, so slim and small,
Crept into a hole beneath the wall;
"Squeak," quoth she, "I'm out of it all."

The Little Bull-Calf

Centuries of years ago, when almost all this part of the country was wilderness, there was a little boy, who lived in a poor bit of property and his father gave him a little bull-calf, and with it he gave him everything he wanted for it.

But soon after his father died, and his mother got married again to a man that turned out to be a very vicious step-father, who couldn't abide the little boy. So at last the step-father said: "If you bring that bull-calf into this house, I'll kill it." What a villain he was, wasn't he?

Now this little boy used to go out and feed his bull-calf every day with barley bread, and when he did so this time, an old man came up to him—we can guess who that was, eh?—and said to him: "You and your bull-calf had better go away and seek your fortune."

So he went on and he went on and he went on, as far as I could tell you till to-morrow night, and he went up to a farmhouse and begged a crust of bread, and when he got back he broke it in two and gave half of it to the bull-calf. And he went to another house and begged a bit of cheese crud, and when he went back he wanted to give half of it to the bull-calf. "No," says the bull-calf, "I'm going across the field, into the wild-wood wilderness country, where there'll be tigers, leopards, wolves, monkeys, and a fiery dragon, and I'll kill them all except the fiery dragon, and he'll kill me."

The little boy did cry, and said: "Oh, no, my little bull-calf; I hope he won't kill you."

"Yes, he will," said the little bull-calf, "so you climb up that tree, so that no one can come nigh you but the monkeys, and if they come the cheese crud will save you. And when I'm killed, the dragon will go away for a bit, then you must come down the tree and skin me, and take out my bladder and blow it out, and it will kill everything you hit with it. So when the fiery dragon comes back, you hit it with my bladder and cut its tongue out."

(We know there were fiery dragons in those days, like George and his dragon in the legend; but, there! it's not the same world nowadays. The world is turned topsy-turvy since then, like as if you'd turn it over with a spade!)

Of course, he did all the little bull-calf told him. He climbed up the tree, and the monkeys climbed up the tree after him. But he held the cheese crud in his hand, and said: "I'll squeeze your heart like the flint-stone." So the monkey cocked his eye as much as to say: "If you can squeeze a flint-stone to make the juice come out of it, you can squeeze me." But he didn't say anything, for a monkey's cunning, but down he went. And all the while the little bull-calf was fighting all the wild beasts on the ground, and the little lad was clapping his hands up the tree, and calling out: "Go in, my little bull-calf! Well fought, little bull-calf!" And he mastered everything except the fiery dragon, but the fiery dragon killed the little bull-calf.

But the lad waited and waited till he saw the dragon go away, then he came down and skinned the little bull-calf, and took out its bladder and went after the dragon. And as he went on, what should he see but a king's daughter, staked down by the hair of her head, for she had been put there for the dragon to destroy her.

So he went up and untied her hair, but she said: "My time has come for the dragon to destroy me; go away, you can do no good." But he said: "No! I can master it, and I won't go"; and for all her begging and praying he would stop.

And soon he heard it coming, roaring and raging from afar off, and at last it came near, spitting fire, and with a tongue like a great spear, and you could hear it roaring for miles, and it was making for the place where the king's daughter was staked down. But when it came up to them, the lad just hit it on the head with the bladder and the dragon fell down dead, but before it died, it bit off the little boy's forefinger.

THE LITTLE BULL-CALF

Then the lad cut out the dragon's tongue and said to the king's daughter: "I've done all I can, I must leave you." And sorry she was he had to go, and before he went she tied a diamond ring in his hair, and said good-bye to him.

By-and-by, who should come along but the old king, lamenting and weeping, expecting to see nothing of his daughter but the prints of the place where she had been. But he was surprised to find her there alive and safe, and he said: "How came you to be saved?" So she told him how she had been saved, and he took her home to his castle again.

Well, he put it into all the papers to find out who saved his daughter, and who had the dragon's tongue and the princess's diamond ring, and was without his forefinger. Whoever could show these signs should marry his daughter and have his kingdom after his death. Well, any number of gentlemen came from all parts of England, with forefingers cut off, and with diamond rings and all kinds of tongues, wild beasts' tongues and foreign tongues. But they couldn't show any dragons' tongues, so they were turned away.

At last the little boy turned up, looking very ragged and desolated like, and the king's daughter cast her eye on him, till her father grew very angry and ordered them to turn the little beggar boy away. "Father," says she; "I know something of that boy."

Well, still the fine gentlemen came, bringing up their dragons' tongues that weren't dragons' tongues, and at last the little boy came up, dressed a little better. So the old king says: "I see you've got an eye on that boy. If it has to be him it must be him." But all the others were fit to kill him, and cried out: "Pooh, pooh, turn that boy out, it can't be him." But the king said: "Now, my boy, let's see what you have to show." Well, he showed the diamond ring with her name on it, and the fiery dragon's tongue. How the others were thunderstruck when he showed his proofs! But the king told him: "You shall have my daughter and my estate."

So he married the princess, and afterwards got the king's estate. Then his step-father came and wanted to own him, but the young king didn't know such a man.

The Wee, Wee Mannie

Once upon a time, when all big folks were wee ones and all lies were true, there was a wee, wee Mannie that had a big, big Coo. And out he went to milk her of a morning, and said—

"Hold still, my Coo, my hinny,
Hold still, my hinny, my Coo,
And ye shall have for your dinner
What but a milk white doo."

But the big, big Coo wouldn't hold still. "Hout!" said the wee, wee Mannie—

"Hold still, my Coo, my dearie,
And fill my bucket wi' milk,
And if ye 'll be no contrairy
I'll gi'e ye a gown o' silk."

But the big, big Coo wouldn't hold still. "Look at that, now!" said the wee, wee Mannie—

"What's a wee, wee mannie to do,
Wi' such a big contrairy Coo?"

So off he went to his mother at the house. "Mother," said he, "Coo won't stand still, and wee, wee Mannie can't milk big, big Coo."

"Hout!" says his mother, "take stick and beat Coo."

So off he went to get a stick from the tree, and said—

"Break, stick, break,
And I'll gi'e ye a cake."

But the stick wouldn't break, so back he went to the house. "Mother," says he, "Coo won't hold still, stick won't break, wee, wee Mannie can't beat big, big Coo."

"Hout!" says his mother, "go to the Butcher and bid him kill Coo."

So off he went to the Butcher, and said—

"Butcher, kill the big, big Coo,
She'll gi'e us no more milk noo."

But the Butcher wouldn't kill the Coo without a silver penny, so back the Mannie went to the house. "Mother," says he, "Coo won't hold still, stick won't break, Butcher won't kill without a silver penny, and wee, wee Mannie can't milk big, big Coo."

"Well," said his mother, "go to the Coo and tell her there's a weary, weary lady with long yellow hair weeping for a cup o' milk."

So off he went and told the Coo, but she wouldn't hold still, so back he went and told his mother.

"Well," said she, "tell the Coo there's a fine, fine laddie from the wars sitting by the weary, weary lady with golden hair, and she weeping for a sup o' milk."

So off he went and told the Coo, but she wouldn't hold still, so back he went and told his mother.

"Well," said his mother, "tell the big, big Coo there's a sharp, sharp sword at the belt of the fine, fine laddie from the wars who sits beside the weary, weary lady with the golden hair, and she weeping for a sup o' milk."

And he told the big, big Coo, but she wouldn't hold still.

Then said his mother, "Run quick and tell her that her head's going to be cut off by the sharp, sharp sword in the hands of the fine, fine laddie, if she doesn't give the sup o' milk the weary, weary lady weeps for."

And wee, wee Mannie went off and told the big, big Coo.

And when Coo saw the glint of the sharp, sharp sword in the hand of the fine, fine laddie come from the wars, and the weary, weary lady weeping for a sup o' milk, she reckoned she'd better hold still; so wee, wee Mannie milked big, big Coo, and the weary, weary lady with the golden hair hushed her weeping and got her sup o' milk, and the fine, fine laddie new come from the wars put by his sharp, sharp sword, and all went well that didn't go ill.

Habetrot and Scantlie Mab

A woman had one fair daughter, who loved play better than work, wandering in the meadows and lanes better than the spinning-wheel and distaff. The mother was heartily vexed at this, for in those days no lassie had any chance of a good husband unless she was an industrious spinster. So she coaxed, threatened, even beat her daughter, but all to no purpose; the girl remained what her mother called her, "an idle cuttie."

At last, one spring morning, the gudewife gave her seven heads of lint, saying she would take no excuse; they must be returned in three days spun into yarn. The girl saw her mother was in earnest, so she plied her distaff as well as she could; but her hands were all untaught, and by the evening of the second day only a very small part of her task was done. She cried herself to sleep that night, and in the morning, throwing aside her work in despair, she strolled out into the fields, all sparkling with dew. At last she reached a knoll, at whose feet ran a little burn, shaded with woodbine and wild roses; and there she sat down, burying her face in her hands. When she looked up, she was surprised to see by the margin of the stream an old woman, quite unknown to her, drawing out the thread as she basked in the sun. There was nothing very remarkable in her appearance, except the length and thickness of her lips, only she was seated on a self-bored stone. The girl rose, went to the good dame, and gave her a friendly greeting, but could not help inquiring "What makes you so long lipped?"

"Spinning thread, my hinnie," said the old woman, pleased with her. "I wet my fingers with my lips, as I draw the thread from the distaff."

"Ah!" said the girl, "I should be spinning too, but it's all to no purpose. I shall ne'er do my task:" on which the old woman proposed to do it for her. Overjoyed, the maiden ran to fetch her lint, and placed it in her new friend's hand, asking where she should call for the yarn in the evening; but she received no reply; the old woman passed away from her among the trees and bushes. The girl, much bewildered, wandered about a little, sat down to rest, and finally fell asleep by the little knoll.

When she awoke she was surprised to find that it was evening. Causleen, the evening star, was beaming with silvery light, soon to be lost in the moon's splendour. While watching these changes, the maiden was startled by the sound of an uncouth voice, which seemed to issue from below the self-bored stone, close beside her. She laid her ear to the stone and heard the words: "Hurry up, Scantlie Mab, for I've promised the yarn and Habetrot always keeps her promise." Then looking down the hole saw her friend, the old dame, walking backwards and forwards in a deep cavern among a group of spinsters all seated on colludie stones, and busy with distaff and spindle. An ugly company they were, with lips more or less disfigured, like old Habetrot's. Another of the sisterhood, who sat in a distant corner reeling the yarn, was marked, in addition, by grey eyes, which seemed starting from her head, and a long hooked nose.

While the girl was still watching, she heard Habetrot address this dame by the name of Scantlie Mab, and say, "Bundle up the yarn, it is time the young lassie should give it to her mother." Delighted to hear this, the girl got up and returned homewards. Habetrot soon overtook her, and placed the yarn in her hands. "Oh, what can I do for ye in return?"

exclaimed she, in delight. "Nothing—nothing," replied the dame; "but dinna tell your mother who spun the yarn."

Scarcely believing her eyes, the girl went home, where she found her mother had been busy making sausters, and hanging them up in the chimney to dry, and then, tired out, had retired to rest. Finding herself very hungry after her long day on the knoll, the girl took down pudding after pudding, fried and ate them, and at last went to bed too. The mother was up first the next morning, and when she came into the kitchen and found her sausters all gone, and the seven hanks of yarn lying beautifully smooth and bright upon the table, she ran out of the house wildly, crying out—

"My daughter's spun seven, seven, seven,
My daughter's eaten seven, seven, seven,
And all before daylight."

A laird who chanced to be riding by, heard the exclamation, but could not understand it; so he rode up and asked the gudewife what was the matter, on which she broke out again—

"My daughter's spun seven, seven, seven,
My daughter's eaten seven, seven, seven

before daylight; and if ye dinna believe me, why come in and see it." The laird, he alighted and went into the cottage, where he saw the yarn, and admired it so much he begged to see the spinner.

The mother dragged in her girl. He vowed he was lonely without a wife, and had long been in search of one who was a good spinner. So their troth was plighted, and the wedding took place soon afterwards, though the bride was in great fear that she should not prove so clever at her spinning-wheel as he expected. But old Dame Habetrot came to her aid. "Bring your bonny bridegroom to my cell," said she to the young bride soon after her marriage; "he shall see what comes o' spinning, and never will he tie you to the spinning-wheel."

Accordingly the bride led her husband the next day to the flowery knoll, and bade him look through the self-bored stone. Great was his surprise to behold Habetrot dancing and jumping over her rock, singing all the time this ditty to her sisterhood, while they kept time with their spindles:—

"We who live in dreary den,
Are both rank and foul to see?
Hidden from the glorious sun,
That teems the fair earth's canopie:
Ever must our evenings lone
Be spent on the colludie stone.

"Cheerless is the evening grey
When Causleen hath died away,
But ever bright and ever fair

Are they who breathe this evening air,
And lean upon the self-bored stone
Unseen by all but me alone."

The song ended, Scantlie Mab asked Habetrot what she meant by the last line, "Unseen by all but we alone."

"There is one," replied Habetrot, "whom I bid to come here at this hour, and he has heard my song through the self-bored stone." So saying she rose, opened another door, which was concealed by the roots of an old tree, and invited the pair to come in and see her family.

The laird was astonished at the weird-looking company, as he well might be, and inquired of one after another the cause of their strange lips. In a different tone of voice, and with a different twist of the mouth, each answered that it was occasioned by spinning. At least they tried to say so, but one grunted out "Nakasind," and another "Owkasaänd," while a third murmured "O-a-a-send." All, however, made the bridegroom understand what was the cause of their ugliness; while Habetrot slily hinted that if his wife were allowed to spin, her pretty lips would grow out of shape too, and her pretty face get an ugsome look. So before he left the cave he vowed that his little wife should never touch a spinning-wheel, and he kept his word. She used to wander in the meadows by his side, or ride behind him over the hills, but all the flax grown on his land was sent to old Habetrot to be converted into yarn.

Old Mother Wiggle-Waggle

The fox and his wife they had a great strife,
They never ate mustard in all their whole life;
They ate their meat without fork or knife
And loved to be picking a bone, e-ho!

The fox went out, one still, clear night,
And he prayed the moon to give him light,
For he'd a long way to travel that night,
Before he got back to his den-o!

The fox when he came to yonder stile,
He lifted his lugs and he listened a while!
"Oh, ho!" said the fox, "it's but a short mile
From this unto yonder wee town, e-ho!"

And first he arrived at a farmer's yard,
Where the ducks and the geese declared it was hard,
That their nerves should be shaken and their rest should be marred
By the visits of Mister Fox-o!

The fox when he came to the farmer's gate,
Who should he see but the farmer's drake;
"I love you well for your master's sake,
And long to be picking your bones, e-ho!"

The grey goose she ran round the hay-stack,
"Oh, ho!" said the fox, "you are very fat;
You'll grease my beard and ride on my back
From this into yonder wee town, e-ho!"

Then he took the grey goose by her sleeve,
And said: "Madam Grey Goose, by your leave
I'll take you away without reprieve,
And carry you back to my den-o!"

And he seized the black duck by the neck,
And slung him all across his back,
The black duck cried out "quack, quack, quack,"
With his legs all dangling down-o!

Old Mother Wiggle-Waggle hopped out of bed,
Out of the window she popped her old head;
"Oh! husband, oh! husband, the grey goose is gone,

And the fox is off to his den, oh!"

Then the old man got up in his red cap,
And swore he would catch the fox in a trap;
But the fox was too cunning, and gave him the slip,
And ran through the town, the town, oh!

When he got to the top of the hill,
He blew his trumpet both loud and shrill,
For joy that he was safe and sound
Through the town, oh!

But at last he arrived at his home again,
To his dear little foxes, eight, nine, ten,
Says he "You're in luck, here's a fine fat duck
With his legs all dangling down-o!"

So he sat down together with his hungry wife,
And they did very well without fork or knife,
They never ate a better duck in all their life,
And the little ones picked the bones-o!

Catskin

Well, there was once a gentleman who had fine lands and houses, and he very much wanted to have a son to be heir to them. So when his wife brought him a daughter, bonny as bonny could be, he cared nought for her, and said, "Let me never see her face."

So she grew up a bonny girl, though her father never set eyes on her till she was fifteen years old and was ready to be married. But her father said, "Let her marry the first that comes for her." And when this was known, who should be first but a nasty rough old man. So she didn't know what to do, and went to the henwife and asked her advice. The henwife said, "Say you will not take him unless they give you a coat of silver cloth." Well, they gave her a coat of silver cloth, but she wouldn't take him for all that, but went again to the henwife, who said, "Say you will not take him unless they give you a coat of beaten gold." Well, they gave her a coat of beaten gold, but still she would not take him, but went to the henwife, who said, "Say you will not take him unless they give you a coat made of the feathers of all the birds of the air." So they sent a man with a great heap of pease; and the man cried to all the birds of the air, "Each bird take a pea, and put down a feather." So each bird took a pea and put down one of its feathers: and they took all the feathers and made a coat of them and gave it to her; but still she would not, but asked the henwife once again, who said, "Say they must first make you a coat of catskin." So they made her a coat of catskin; and she put it on, and tied up her other coats, and ran away into the woods.

So she went along and went along and went along, till she came to the end of the wood, and saw a fine castle. So there she hid her fine dresses, and went up to the castle gates, and asked for work. The lady of the castle saw her, and told her, "I'm sorry I have no better place, but if you like you may be our scullion." So down she went into the kitchen, and they called her Catskin, because of her dress. But the cook was very cruel to her and led her a sad life.

Well, it happened soon after that the young lord of the castle was coming home, and there was to be a grand ball in honour of the occasion. And when they were speaking about it among the servants, "Dear me, Mrs. Cook," said Catskin, "how much I should like to go."

"What! you dirty impudent slut," said the cook, "you go among all the fine lords and ladies with your filthy catskin? a fine figure you'd cut!" and with that she took a basin of water and dashed it into Catskin's face. But she only briskly shook her ears, and said nothing.

When the day of the ball arrived, Catskin slipped out of the house and went to the edge of the forest where she had hidden her dresses. So she bathed herself in a crystal waterfall, and then put on her coat of silver cloth, and hastened away to the ball. As soon as she entered all were overcome by her beauty and grace, while the young lord at once lost his heart to her. He asked her to be his partner for the first dance, and he would dance with none other the live-long night.

When it came to parting time, the young lord said, "Pray tell me, fair maid, where you live." But Catskin curtsied and said:

"Kind sir, if the truth I must tell,
At the sign of the 'Basin of Water' I dwell."

Then she flew from the castle and donned her catskin robe again, and slipped into the scullery again, unbeknown to the cook.

The young lord went the very next day to his mother, the lady of the castle, and declared he would wed none other but the lady of the silver dress, and would never rest till he had found her. So another ball was soon arranged for in hope that the beautiful maid would appear again. So Catskin said to the cook, "Oh, how I should like to go!" Whereupon the cook screamed out in a rage, "What, you, you dirty impudent slut! you would cut a fine figure among all the fine lords and ladies." And with that she up with a ladle and broke it across Catskin's back. But she only shook her ears, and ran off to the forest, where she first of all bathed, and then put on her coat of beaten gold, and off she went to the ball-room.

As soon as she entered all eyes were upon her; and the young lord soon recognised her as the lady of the "Basin of Water," and claimed her hand for the first dance, and did not leave her till the last. When that came, he again asked her where she lived. But all that she would say was:

"Kind sir, if the truth I must tell,
At the sign of the 'Broken Ladle' I dwell."

and with that she curtsied, and flew from the ball, off with her golden robe, on with her catskin, and into the scullery without the cook's knowing.

Next day when the young lord could not find where was the sign of the "Basin of Water," or of the "Broken Ladle," he begged his mother to have another grand ball, so that he might meet the beautiful maid once more.

All happened as before. Catskin told the cook how much she would like to go to the ball, the cook called her "a dirty slut," and broke the skimmer across her head. But she only shook her ears, and went off to the forest, where she first bathed in the crystal spring, and then donned her coat of feathers, and so off to the ball-room.

When she entered every one was surprised at so beautiful a face and form dressed in so rich and rare a dress; but the young lord soon recognised his beautiful sweetheart, and would dance with none but her the whole evening. When the ball came to an end, he pressed her to tell him where she lived, but all she would answer was:

"Kind sir, if the truth I must tell,
At the sign of the 'Broken Skimmer' I dwell;"

and with that she curtsied, and was off to the forest. But this time the young lord followed her, and watched her change her fine dress of feathers for her catskin dress, and then he knew her for his own scullery-maid.

Next day he went to his mother, the lady of the castle, and told her that he wished to marry the scullery-maid, Catskin. "Never," said the lady, and rushed from the room. Well, the young lord was so grieved at that, that he took to his bed and was very ill. The doctor tried to cure him, but he would not take any medicine unless from the hands of Catskin. So the doctor went to the lady of the castle, and told her her son would die if she did not consent to his marriage with Catskin. So she had to give way, and summoned Catskin to her. But she put on her coat of beaten gold, and went to the lady, who soon was glad to wed her son to so beautiful a maid.

Well, so they were married, and after a time a dear little son came to them, and grew up a bonny lad; and one day, when he was four years old, a beggar woman came to the door, so Lady Catskin gave some money to the little lord and told him to go and give it to the beggar woman. So he went and gave it, but put it into the hand of the woman's child, who leant forward and kissed the little lord. Now the wicked old cook—why hadn't she been sent away?—was looking on, so she said, "Only see how beggars' brats take to one another." This insult went to Catskin's heart, so she went to her husband, the young lord, and told him all about her father, and begged he would go and find out what had become of her parents. So they set out in the lord's grand coach, and travelled through the forest till they came to Catskin's father's house, and put up at an inn near, where Catskin stopped, while her husband went to see if her father would own her.

Now her father had never had any other child, and his wife had died; so he was all alone in the world and sate moping and miserable. When the young lord came in he hardly looked up, till he saw a chair close up to him, and asked him: "Pray, sir, had you not once a young daughter whom you would never see or own?"

The old gentleman said: "It is true; I am a hardened sinner. But I would give all my worldly goods if I could but see her once before I die." Then the young lord told him what had happened to Catskin, and took him to the inn, and brought his father-in-law to his own castle, where they lived happy ever afterwards.

Stupid's Cries

There was once a little boy, and his mother sent him to buy a sheep's head and pluck; afraid he should forget it, the lad kept saying all the way along:

"Sheep's head and pluck!
Sheep's head and pluck!"

Trudging along, he came to a stile; but in getting over he fell and hurt himself, and beginning to blubber, forgot what he was sent for. So he stood a little while to consider: at last he thought he recollected it, and began to repeat:

"Liver and lights and gall and all!
Liver and lights and gall and all!"

Away he went again, and came to where a man had a pain in his liver, bawling out:

"Liver and lights and gall and all!
Liver and lights and gall and all!"

Whereon the man laid hold of him and beat him, bidding him say:

"Pray God send no more!
Pray God send no more!"

The youngster strode along, uttering these words, till he reached a field where a hind was sowing wheat:

"Pray God send no more!
Pray God send no more!"

This was all his cry. So the sower began to thrash him, and charged him to repeat:

"Pray God send plenty more!
Pray God send plenty more!"

Off the child scampered with these words in his mouth till he reached a churchyard and met a funeral, but he went on with his:

"Pray God send plenty more!
Pray God send plenty more!"

The chief mourner seized and punished him, and bade him repeat:

"Pray God send the soul to heaven!
Pray God send the soul to heaven!"

Away went the boy, and met a dog and a cat going to be hung, but his cry rang out:

"Pray God send the soul to heaven!
Pray God send the soul to heaven!"

The good folk nearly were furious, seized and struck him, charging him to say:

"A dog and a cat agoing to be hung!
A dog and a cat agoing to be hung!"

This the poor fellow did, till he overtook a man and a woman going to be married. "Oh! oh!" he shouted:

"A dog and a cat agoing to be hung!
A dog and a cat agoing to be hung!"

The man was enraged, as we may well think, gave him many a thump, and ordered him to repeat:

"I wish you much joy!
I wish you much joy!"

This he did, jogging along, till he came to two labourers who had fallen into a ditch. The lad kept bawling out:

"I wish you much joy!
I wish you much joy!"

This vexed one of the folk so sorely that he used all his strength, scrambled out, beat the crier, and told him to say.

"The one is out, I wish the other was!
The one is out, I wish the other was!"

On went young 'un till he found a fellow with only one eye; but he kept up his song:

"The one is out, I wish the other was!
The one is out, I wish the other was!"

This was too much for Master One-eye, who grabbed him and chastised him, bidding him call:

"The one side gives good light, I wish the other did!
The one side gives good light, I wish the other did!"

So he did, to be sure, till he came to a house, one side of which was on fire. The people here thought it was he who had set the place a-blazing, and straightway put him in prison. The end was, the judge put on his black cap, and condemned him to die.

The Lambton Worm

A wild young fellow was the heir of Lambton, the fine estate and hall by the side of the swift-flowing Wear. Not a Mass would he hear in Brugeford Chapel of a Sunday, but a-fishing he would go. And if he did not haul in anything, his curses could be heard by the folk as they went by to Brugeford.

Well, one Sunday morning he was fishing as usual, and not a salmon had risen to him, his basket was bare of roach or dace. And the worse his luck, the worse grew his language, till the passers-by were horrified at his words as they went to listen to the Mass-priest.

At last young Lambton felt a mighty tug at his line. "At last," quoth he, "a bite worth having!" and he pulled and he pulled, till what should appear above the water but a head like an elf's, with nine holes on each side of its mouth. But still he pulled till he had got the thing to land, when it turned out to be a Worm of hideous shape. If he had cursed before, his curses were enough to raise the hair on your head.

"What ails thee, my son?" said a voice by his side, "and what hast thou caught, that thou shouldst stain the Lord's Day with such foul language?"

Looking round, young Lambton saw a strange old man standing by him.

"Why, truly," he said, "I think I have caught the devil himself. Look you and see if you know him."

But the stranger shook his head, and said, "It bodes no good to thee or thine to bring such a monster to shore. Yet cast him not back into the Wear; thou has caught him, and thou must keep him," and with that away he turned, and was seen no more.

The young heir of Lambton took up the gruesome thing, and, taking it off his hook, cast it into a well close by, and ever since that day that well has gone by the name of the Worm Well.

For some time nothing more was seen or heard of the Worm, till one day it had outgrown the size of the well, and came forth full-grown. So it came forth from the well and betook itself to the Wear. And all day long it would lie coiled round a rock in the middle of the stream, while at night it came forth from the river and harried the country side. It sucked the cows' milk, devoured the lambs, worried the cattle, and frightened all the women and girls of the district, and then it would retire for the rest of the night to the hill, still called the Worm Hill, on the north side of the Wear, about a mile and a half from Lambton Hall.

This terrible visitation brought young Lambton, of Lambton Hall, to his senses. He took upon himself the vows of the Cross, and departed for the Holy Land, in the hope that the scourge he had brought upon his district would disappear. But the grisly Worm took no heed, except that it crossed the river and came right up to Lambton Hall itself where the old lord lived on all alone, his only son having gone to the Holy Land. What to do? The Worm was coming closer and closer to the Hall; women were shrieking, men were gathering weapons, dogs were barking and horses neighing with terror. At last the steward called out to the dairy maids, "Bring all your milk hither," and when they did so, and had brought all the milk that the nine kye of the byre had yielded, he poured it all into the long stone trough in front of the Hall.

The Worm drew nearer and nearer, till at last it came up to the trough. But when it sniffed the milk, it turned aside to the trough and swallowed all the milk up, and then slowly turned round and crossed the river Wear, and coiled its bulk three times round the Worm Hill for the night.

Henceforth the Worm would cross the river every day, and woe betide the Hall if the trough contained the milk of less than nine kye. The Worm would hiss, and would rave, and lash its tail round the trees of the park, and in its fury it would uproot the stoutest oaks and the loftiest firs. So it went on for seven years. Many tried to destroy the Worm, but all had failed, and many a knight had lost his life in fighting with the monster, which slowly crushed the life out of all that came near it.

At last the Childe of Lambton came home to his father's Hall, after seven long years spent in meditation and repentance on holy soil. Sad and desolate he found his folk: the lands untilled, the farms deserted, half the trees of the park uprooted, for none would stay to tend the nine kye that the monster needed for his food each day.

The Childe sought his father, and begged his forgiveness for the curse he had brought on the Hall.

"Thy sin is pardoned," said his father; "but go thou to the Wise Woman of Brugeford, and find if aught can free us from this monster."

To the Wise Woman went the Childe, and asked her advice.

"'T is thy fault, O Childe, for which we suffer," she said; "be it thine to release us."

"I would give my life," said the Childe.

"Mayhap thou wilt do so," said she. "But hear me, and mark me well. Thou, and thou alone, canst kill the Worm. But, to this end, go thou to the smithy and have thy armour studded with spear-heads. Then go to the Worm's Rock in the Wear, and station thyself there. Then, when the Worm comes to the Rock at dawn of day, try thy prowess on him, and God gi'e thee a good deliverance."

"This I will do," said Childe Lambton.

"But one thing more," said the Wise Woman, going back to her cell. "If thou slay the Worm, swear that thou wilt put to death the first thing that meets thee as thou crossest again the threshold of Lambton Hall. Do this, and all will be well with thee and thine. Fulfil not thou vow, and none of the Lambtons, for generations three times three, shall die in his bed. Swear, and fail not."

The Childe swore as the Wise Woman bid, and went his way to the smithy. There he had his armour studded with spear-heads all over. Then he passed his vigils in Brugeford Chapel, and at dawn of day took his post on the Worm's Rock in the River Wear.

As dawn broke, the Worm uncoiled its snaky twine from around the hill, and came to its rock in the river. When it perceived the Childe waiting for it, it lashed the waters in its fury and wound its coils round the Childe, and then attempted to crush him to death. But the more it pressed, the deeper dug the spear-heads into its sides. Still it pressed and pressed, till all the water around was crimsoned with its blood. Then the Worm unwound itself, and left the Childe free to use his sword. He raised it, brought it down, and cut the Worm in two. One half fell into the river, and was carried swiftly away. Once more the head and the remainder of the body encircled the Childe, but with less force, and the spear-heads did their work. At last the Worm uncoiled itself, snorted its last foam of blood and fire, and rolled dying into the river, and was never seen more.

THE LAMBTON WORM

The Childe of Lambton swam ashore, and raising his bugle to his lips, sounded its note thrice. This was the signal to the Hall, where the servants and the old lord had shut themselves in to pray for the Childe's success. When the third sound of the bugle was heard, they were to release Boris, the Childe's favourite hound. But such was their joy at learning of the Childe's safety and the Worm's defeat, that they forgot orders, and when the Childe reached the threshold of the Hall his old father rushed out to meet him, and would have clasped him to his breast.

"The vow! the vow!" cried out the Childe of Lambton, and blew still another blast upon his horn. This time the servants remembered, and released Boris, who came bounding to his young master. The Childe raised his shining sword, and severed the head of his faithful hound.

But the vow was broken, and for nine generations of men none of the Lambtons died in his bed. The last of the Lambtons died in his carriage as he was crossing Brugeford Bridge, one hundred and thirty years ago.

The Wise Men of Gotham

Of Buying of Sheep

There were two men of Gotham, and one of them was going to market to Nottingham to buy sheep, and the other came from the market, and they both met together upon Nottingham bridge.

"Where are you going?" said the one who came from Nottingham.

"Marry," said he that was going to Nottingham, "I am going to buy sheep."

"Buy sheep?" said the other, "and which way will you bring them home?"

"Marry," said the other, "I will bring them over this bridge."

"By Robin Hood," said he that came from Nottingham, "but thou shalt not."

"By Maid Marion," said he that was going thither, "but I will."

"You will not," said the one.

"I will."

Then they beat their staves against the ground one against the other, as if there had been a hundred sheep between them.

"Hold in," said one; "beware lest my sheep leap over the bridge."

"I care not," said the other; "they shall not come this way."

"But they shall," said the other.

Then the other said: "If that thou make much to do, I will put my fingers in thy mouth."

"Will you?" said the other.

Now, as they were at their contention, another man of Gotham came from the market with a sack of meal upon a horse, and seeing and hearing his neighbours at strife about sheep, though there were none between them, said:

"Ah, fools! will you ever learn wisdom? Help me, and lay my sack upon my shoulders."

They did so, and he went to the side of the bridge, unloosened the mouth of the sack, and shook all his meal out into the river.

"Now, neighbours," he said, "how much meal is there in my sack?"

"Marry," said they, "there is none at all."

"Now, by my faith," said he, "even as much wit as is in your two heads to stir up strife about a thing you have not."

Which was the wisest of these three persons, judge yourself.

Of Hedging a Cuckoo

Once upon a time the men of Gotham would have kept the Cuckoo so that she might sing all the year, and in the midst of their town they made a hedge round in compass and they got a Cuckoo, and put her into it, and said, "Sing there all through the year, or thou shalt have neither meat nor water." The Cuckoo, as soon as she perceived herself within the hedge, flew away. "A vengeance on her!" said they. "We did not make our hedge high enough."

Of Sending Cheeses

There was a man of Gotham who went to the market at Nottingham to sell cheese, and as he was going down the hill to Nottingham bridge, one of his cheeses fell out of his wallet and rolled down the hill. "Ah, gaffer," said the fellow, "can you run to market alone? I will send one after another after you."

Then he laid down his wallet and took out the cheeses, and rolled them down the hill. Some went into one bush; and some went into another.

"I charge you all to meet me near the market-place;" and when the fellow came to the market to meet his cheeses, he stayed there till the market was nearly done. Then he went about to inquire of his friends and neighbours, and other men, if they did see his cheeses come to the market.

"Who should bring them?" said one of the market men.

"Marry, themselves," said the fellow; "they know the way well enough."

He said, "A vengeance on them all. I did fear, to see them run so fast, that they would run beyond the market. I am now fully persuaded that they must be now almost at York." Whereupon he forthwith hired a horse to ride to York, to seek his cheeses where they were not, but to this day no man can tell him of his cheeses.

Of Drowning Eels

When Good Friday came, the men of Gotham cast their heads together what to do with their white herrings, their red herrings, their sprats, and other salt fish. One consulted with the other, and agreed that such fish should be cast into their pond (which was in the middle of the town), that they might breed against the next year, and every man that had salt fish left cast them into the pool.

"I have many white herrings," said one.

"I have many sprats," said another.

"I have many red herrings," said the other.

"I have much salt fish. Let all go into the pond or pool, and we shall fare like lords next year."

At the beginning of next year following the men drew near the pond to have their fish, and there was nothing but a great eel. "Ah," said they all, "a mischief on this eel, for he has eaten up all our fish."

"What shall we do to him?" said one to the others.

"Kill him," said one.

"Chop him into pieces," said another. "Not so," said another; "let us drown him."

"Be it so," said all. And they went to another pond, and cast the eel into the pond. "Lie there and shift for yourself, for no help thou shalt have from us;" and they left the eel to drown.

Of Sending Rent

Once on a time the men of Gotham had forgotten to pay their landlord. One said to the other, "To-morrow is our pay-day, and what shall we find to send our money to our landlord?"

The one said, "This day I have caught a hare, and he shall carry it, for he is light of foot."

"Be it so," said all; "he shall have a letter and a purse to put our money in, and we shall direct him the right way." So when the letters were written and the money put in a purse, they tied it round the hare's neck, saying, "First you go to Lancaster, then thou must go to Loughborough, and Newarke is our landlord, and commend us to him and there is his dues."

The hare, as soon as he was out of their hands, ran on along the country way. Some cried, "Thou must go to Lancaster first."

"Let the hare alone," said another; "he can tell a nearer way than the best of us all. Let him go."

Another said, "It is a subtle hare, let her alone; she will not keep the highway for fear of dogs."

Of Counting

On a certain time there were twelve men of Gotham who went fishing, and some went into the water and some on dry ground; and, as they were coming back, one of them said, "We have ventured much this day wading; I pray God that none of us that did come from home be drowned."

"Marry," said one, "let us see about that. Twelve of us came out," and every man did count eleven, and the twelfth man did never count himself.

"Alas!" said one to another, "one of us is drowned." They went back to the brook where they had been fishing, and looked up and down for him that was drowned, and made great lamentation. A courtier came riding by, and he did ask what they were seeking, and why they were so sorrowful. "Oh," said they, "this day we came to fish in this brook, and there were twelve of us, and one is drowned."

"Why," said the courtier, "count me how many of you there be," and one counted eleven and did not count himself. "Well," said the courtier, "what will you give me if I find the twelfth man?"

"Sir," said they, "all the money we have."

"Give me the money," said the courtier; and he began with the first, and gave him a whack over the shoulders that he groaned, and said, "There is one," and he served all of them that they groaned; but when he came to the last he gave him a good blow, saying, "Here is the twelfth man."

"God bless you on your heart," said all the company; "you have found our neighbour."

Princess of Canterbury

There lived formerly in the County of Cumberland a nobleman who had three sons, two of whom were comely and clever youths, but the other a natural fool, named Jack, who was generally engaged with the sheep: he was dressed in a parti-coloured coat, and a steeple-crowned hat with a tassel, as became his condition. Now the King of Canterbury had a beautiful daughter, who was distinguished by her great ingenuity and wit, and he issued a decree that whoever should answer three questions put to him by the princess should have her in marriage, and be heir to the crown at his decease. Shortly after this decree was published, news of it reached the ears of the nobleman's sons, and the two clever ones determined to have a trial, but they were sadly at a loss to prevent their idiot brother from going with them. They could not, by any means, get rid of him, and were compelled at length to let Jack accompany them. They had not gone far, before Jack shrieked with laughter, saying, "I've found an egg." "Put it in your pocket," said the brothers. A little while afterwards, he burst out into another fit of laughter on finding a crooked hazel stick, which he also put in his pocket; and a third time he again laughed extravagantly because he found a nut. That also was put with his other treasures.

When they arrived at the palace, they were immediately admitted on mentioning the nature of their business, and were ushered into a room where the princess and her suite were sitting. Jack, who never stood on ceremony, bawled out, "What a troop of fair ladies we've got here!"

"Yes," said the princess, "we are fair ladies, for we carry fire in our bosoms."

"Do you?" said Jack, "then roast me an egg," pulling out the egg from his pocket.

"How will you get it out again?" said the princess.

"With a crooked stick," replied Jack, producing the hazel.

"Where did that come from?" said the princess.

"From a nut," answered Jack, pulling out the nut from his pocket. "I've answered the three questions, and now I'll have the lady." "No, no," said the king, "not so fast. You have still an ordeal to go through. You must come here in a week's time and watch for one whole night with the princess, my daughter. If you can manage to keep awake the whole night long you shall marry her next day."

"But if I can't?" said Jack.

"Then off goes your head," said the king. "But you need not try unless you like."

Well, Jack went back home for a week, and thought over whether he should try and win the princess. At last he made up his mind. "Well," said Jack, "I'll try my vorton; zo now vor the king's daughter, or a headless shepherd!"

And taking his bottle and bag, he trudged to the court. In his way thither, he was obliged to cross a river, and pulling off his shoes and stockings, while he was passing over he observed several pretty fish bobbing against his feet; so he caught some and put them into his pocket. When he reached the palace he knocked at the gate loudly with his crook, and having mentioned the object of his visit, he was immediately conducted to the hall where the king's daughter sat ready prepared to see her lovers. He was placed in a luxurious chair, and rich wines and spices were set before him, and all sorts of delicate meats. Jack, unused to such fare, ate and drank plentifully, so that he was nearly dozing before midnight.

"Oh, shepherd," said the lady, "I have caught you napping!"

"Noa, sweet ally, I was busy a-feeshing."

"A fishing," said the princess in the utmost astonishment: "Nay, shepherd, there is no fish-pond in the hall."

"No matter vor that, I have been fishing in my pocket, and have just caught one."

"Oh me!" said she, "let me see it."

The shepherd slyly drew the fish out of his pocket and pretending to have caught it, showed it her, and she declared it was the finest she ever saw.

About half an hour afterwards, she said, "Shepherd, do you think you could get me one more?"

He replied, "Mayhap I may, when I have baited my hook;" and after a little while he brought out another, which was finer than the first, and the princess was so delighted that she gave him leave to go to sleep, and promised to excuse him to her father.

In the morning the princess told the king, to his great astonishment, that Jack must not be beheaded, for he had been fishing in the hall all night; but when he heard how Jack had caught such beautiful fish out of his pocket, he asked him to catch one in his own.

Jack readily undertook the task, and bidding the king lie down, he pretended to fish in his pocket, having another fish concealed ready in his hand, and giving him a sly prick with a needle, he held up the fish, and showed it to the king.

His majesty did not much relish the operation, but he assented to the marvel of it, and the princess and Jack were united the same day, and lived for many years in happiness and prosperity.

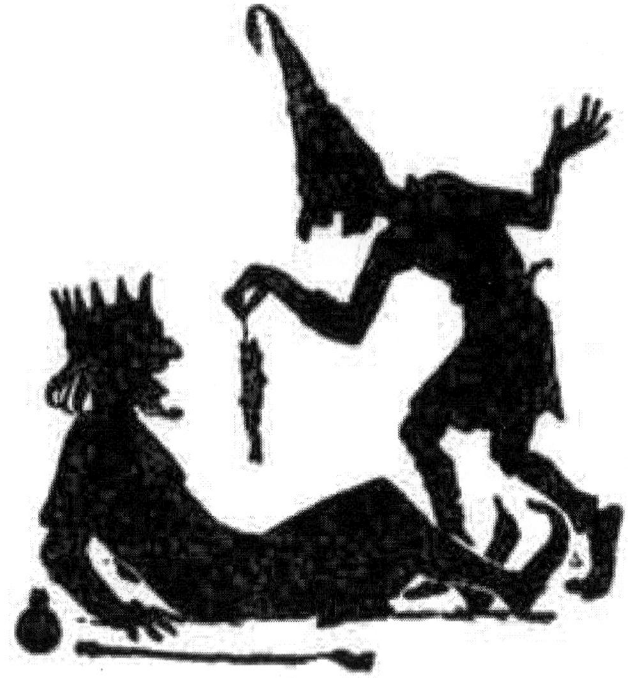

**OYEZ OYEZ OYEZ
THE ENGLISH FAIRY TALES
ARE NOW CLOSED
LITTLE BOYS AND GIRLS
MUST NOT READ ANY FURTHER**

Notes and References

For some general remarks on the English Folk-Tale and previous collectors, I must refer to the introductory observations added to the Notes and References of *English Fairy Tales*, in the third edition. With the present instalment the tale of English Fairy Stories that are likely to obtain currency among the young folk is complete. I do not know of more than half-a-dozen "outsiders" that deserve to rank with those included in my two volumes which, for the present, at any rate, must serve as the best substitute that can be offered for an English Grimm. I do not despair of the future. After what Miss Fison (who, as I have recently learned, was the collector of *Tom Tit Tot* and *Cap o' Rushes*), Mrs. Balfour, and Mrs. Gomme have done in the way of collecting among the folk, we may still hope for substantial additions to our stock to be garnered by ladies from the less frequented portions of English soil. And from the United States we have every reason to expect a rich harvest to be gathered by Mr. W.W. Newell, who is collecting the English folk-tales that still remain current in New England. If his forthcoming book equals in charm, scholarship, and thoroughness his delightful *Games and Songs of American Children*, the Anglo-American folk-tale will be enriched indeed. A further examination of English nursery rhymes may result in some additions to our stock. I reserve these for separate treatment in which I am especially interested, owing to the relations which I surmise between the folk-tale and the *cante-fable*.

Meanwhile the eighty-seven tales (representing some hundred and twenty variants) in my two volumes must represent the English folk-tale as far as my diligence has been able to preserve it at this end of the nineteenth century. There is every indication that they form but a scanty survival of the whole *corpus* of such tales which must have existed in this country. Of the seventy European story-radicles which I have enumerated in the Folk-Lore Society's *Handbook*, pp. 117-35, only forty are represented in our collection: I have little doubt that the majority of the remaining thirty or so also existed in these isles, and especially in England. If I had reckoned in the tales current in the English pale of Ireland, as well as those in Lowland Scots, there would have been even less missing. The result of my investigations confirms me in my impression that the scope of the English folk-tale should include all those current among the folk in English, no matter where spoken, in Ireland, the Lowlands, New England, or Australia. Wherever there is community of language, tales can spread, and it is more likely that tales should be preserved in those parts where English is spoken with most of dialect. Just as the Anglo-Irish Pale preserves more of the pronunciation of Shakespeare's time, so it is probable that Anglo-Irish stories preserve best those current in Shakespeare's time in English. On the other hand, it is possible that some, nay many, of the Anglo-Irish stories have been imported from the Celtic districts, and are positively folk-translations from the Gaelic. Further research is required to determine which is English and which Celtic among Anglo-Irish folk-tales. Meanwhile my collection must stand for the nucleus of the English folk-tale, and we can at any rate judge of its general spirit and tendencies from the eighty-seven tales now before the reader.

Of these, thirty-eight are *märchen* proper, *i.e.*, tales with definite plot and evolution; ten are sagas or legends locating romantic stories in definite localities; no less than nineteen are drolls or comic anecdotes; four are cumulative stories: six beast tales; while ten are merely ingenious nonsense tales put together in such a form as to amuse children. The preponderance of the comic element is marked, and it is clear that humour is a characteristic of the English *folk*. The legends are not of a very romantic kind, and the *märchen* are often humorous in character. So that a certain air of unromance is given by such a collection as that we are here considering. The English folk-muse wears homespun and plods afoot, albeit with a cheerful smile and a steady gaze.

Some of this effect is produced by the manner in which the tales are told. The colloquial manner rarely rises to the dignified, and the essence of the folk-tale manner in English is colloquial. The opening formulæ are varied enough, but none of them has much play of fancy. "Once upon a time and a very good time it was, though it wasn't in my time nor in your time nor in any one else's time," is effective enough for a fairy epoch, and is common, according to Mayhew (*London Labour*. iii.), among tramps. We have the rhyming formula:

Once upon a time when pigs spoke rhyme,
And monkeys chewed tobacco,
And hens took snuff to make them tough,
And ducks went quack, quack, quack Oh!

on which I have variants not so refined. Some stories start off without any preliminary formula, or with a simple "Well, there was once a ———". A Scotch formula reported by Mrs. Balfour runs, "Once on a time when a' muckle folk were wee and a' lees were true," while Mr. Lang gives us "There was a king and a queen as many ane's been, few have we seen and as few may we see." Endings of stories are even less varied. "So they married and lived happy ever afterwards," comes from folk-tales, not from novels. "All went well that didn't go ill," is a somewhat cynical formula given by Mrs. Balfour, while the Scotch have "they lived happy and died happy, and never drank out of a dry cappie."

In the course of the tale the chief thing to be noticed is the occurrence of rhymes in the prose narrative, tending to give the appearance of a *cante-fable*. I have enumerated those occurring in *English Fairy Tales* in the notes to *Childe Rowland* (No. xxi.). In the present volume, rhyme occurs in Nos. xlvi., xlviii., xlix., lviii., lx., lxiii. (see Note), lxiv., lxxiv., lxxxi., lxxxv., while lv., lxix., lxxiii., lxxvi., lxxxiii., lxxxiv., are either in verse themselves or derived from verse versions. Altogether one third of our collection gives evidence in favour of the *cante-fable* theory which I adduced in my notes to *Childe Rowland*. Another point of interest in English folk-narrative is the repetition of verbs of motion, "So he went along and went along and went along." Still more curious is a frequent change of tense from the English present to the past. "So he gets up and went along." All this helps to give the colloquial and familiar air to the English fairy-tale not to mention the dialectal and archaic words and phrases which occur in them.

But their very familiarity and colloquialism make them remarkably effective with English-speaking little ones. The rhythmical phrases stick in their memories; they can remember the exact phraseology of the English tales much better, I find, than that of the Grimms' tales, or even of the Celtic stories. They certainly have the quality of coming home to English children. Perhaps this may be partly due to the fact that a larger proportion of the tales are of native manufacture. If the researches contained in my Notes are to be trusted only i.-ix., xi., xvii., xxii., xxv., xxvi., xxvii., xliv., l., liv., lv., lviii., lxi., lxii., lxv., lxvii., lxxviii., lxxxiv., lxxxvii. were imported; nearly all the remaining sixty are home produce, and have their roots in the hearts of the English people which naturally respond to them.

In the following Notes, I have continued my practice of giving (1) *Source* where I obtained the various tales. (2) *Parallels*, so far as possible, in full for the British Isles, with bibliographical references when they can be found; for occurrences abroad I generally refer to the list of incidents contained in my paper read before the International Folk-Lore Congress of 1891 and republished in the *Transactions*, 1892, pp. 87-98. (3) *Remarks* where the tale seems to need them. I have mainly been on the search for signs of diffusion rather than of "survivals" of antiquarian interest, though I trust it will be found I have not neglected these.

XLIV. THE PIED PIPER

Source.—Abraham Elder, *Tales and Legends of the Isle of Wight* (London, 1839), pp. 157-164. Mr. Nutt, who has abridged and partly rewritten the story from a copy of Elder's book in his possession, has introduced a couple of touches from Browning.

Parallels.—The well-known story of the Pied Piper of Hameln (Hamelin), immortalised by Browning, will at once recur to every reader's mind. Before Browning, it had been told in English in books as well known as Verstegan's *Restitution of Decayed Intelligence*, 1605; Howell's *Familiar Letters* (see my edition, p. 357, *n.*); and Wanley's *Wonders of the Little World*. Browning is said to have taken it from the last source (Furnivall, *Browning Bibliography*, 158), though there are touches which seem to me to come from Howell (see my note *ad loc.*), while it is not impossible he may have come across Elder's book, which was illustrated by Cruikshank. The Grimms give the legend in their *Deutsche Sagen* (ed. 1816, 330-33), and in its native land it has given rise to an elaborate poem *à la* Scheffel by Julius Wolff, which has in its turn been the occasion of an opera by Victor Nessler. Mrs. Gutch, in an interesting study of the myth in *Folk-Lore* iii., pp. 227-52, quotes a poem, *The Sea Piece*, published by Dr. Kirkpatrick in 1750, as showing that a similar legend was told of the Cave Hill, Belfast.

Here, as Tradition's hoary legend tells,
A blinking Piper once with magic Spells
And strains beyond a vulgar Bagpipe's sounds
Gathered the dancing Country wide around.
When hither as he drew the tripping Rear
(Dreadful to think and difficult to swear!)
The gaping Mountain yawned from side to side,
A hideous Cavern, darksome, deep, and wide;
In skipt th' exulting Demon, piping loud,
With passive joy succeeded by the Crowd.
* * * * * * *
There firm and instant closed the greedy Womb,
Where wide-born Thousands met a common Tomb.

Remarks.—Mr. Baring-Gould, in his *Curious Myths of the Middle Ages*, has explained the Pied Piper as a wind myth. Mrs. Gutch is inclined to think there may be a substratum of fact at the root of the legend, basing her conclusions on a pamphlet of Dr. Meinardus, *Der historische Kern*, which I have not seen. She does not, however, give any well-authenticated historical event at Hameln in the thirteenth century which could have plausibly given rise to the legend, nor can I find any in the *Urkundenbuch* of Hameln (Luneberg, 1883). The chief question of interest attaching to the English form of the legend as given in 1839 by Elder, is whether it is independent of the German myth. It does not occur in any of the local histories of the Isle of Wight which I have been able to consult of a date previous to Elder's book—*e.g.*, J. Hassel, *Tour of the Isle of Wight*, 1790. Mr. Shore, in his *History of Hampshire*, 1891, p. 185, refers to the legend, but evidently bases his reference on Elder, and so with all the modern references I have seen. Now Elder himself quotes Verstegan in his comments on the legend, pp. 168-9 and note, and it is impossible to avoid conjecturing that he adapted Verstegan to the locality. Newtown, when Hassel visited it in 1790, had only six or seven houses (*l.c.*, i., 137-8), though it had the privilege of returning two members to Parliament; it had been a populous town by the name of Franchville before the French invasion of the island of *temp*. Ric. II. It is just possible that there may have been a local legend to account for the depopulation by an exodus of the children. But the expression "pied piper" which Elder used clearly came from Verstegan, and until evidence is shown to the contrary the whole of the legend was adapted from him. It is not without significance that Elder was writing in the days of the *Ingoldsby Legends*, and had possibly no more foundation for the localisation of his stories than Barham.

There still remains the curious parallel from Belfast to which Mrs. Gutch has drawn attention. Magic pipers are not unknown to English folk-lore, as in the Percy ballad of *The Frere and the Boy*, or in the nursery rhyme of Tom the Piper's son in its more extended form. But beguiling into a mountain is not known elsewhere except at Hameln, which was made widely known in England by Verstegan's and Howell's accounts, so that the Belfast variant is also probably to be traced to the *Rattenfänger*. Here again, as in the case of Beddgellert (*Celtic Fairy Tales*, No. xxi.), the Blinded Giant and the Pedlar of Swaffham (*infra*, Nos. lxi., lxiii.), we have an imported legend adapted to local conditions.

XLV. HEREAFTERTHIS

Source.—Sent me anonymously soon after the appearance of *English Fairy Tales*. From a gloss in the MS. "vitty" = Devonian for "decent," I conclude the tale is current in Devon. I should be obliged if the sender would communicate with me.

Parallels.—The latter part has a certain similarity with "Jack Hannaford" (No. viii.). Halliwell's story of the miser who kept his money "for luck" (p. 153) is of the same type. Halliwell remarks that the tale throws light on a passage in Ben Jonson:

Say we are robbed,
If any come to borrow a spoon or so

I will not have Good Fortune or God's Blessing
Let in, while I am busy.

The earlier part of the tale has resemblance with "Lazy Jack" (No. xxvii), the European variants of which are given by M. Cosquin, *Contes de Lorraine*, i., 241. Jan's satisfaction with his wife's blunders is also European (Cosquin, *l.c.*, i., 157). On minding the door and dispersing robbers by its aid see "Mr. Vinegar" (No. vi.).

Remarks.—"Hereafterthis" is thus a *mélange* of droll incidents, yet has characteristic folkish touches ("can you milk-y, bake-y," "when I lived home") which give it much vivacity.

XLVI. THE GOLDEN BALL

Source.—Contributed to the first edition of Henderson's *Folk-Lore of the Northern Counties*, pp. 333-5, by Rev. S. Baring-Gould.

Parallels.—Mr. Nutt gave a version in *Folk-Lore Journal*, vi., 144. The man in instalments occurs in "The Strange Visitor" (No. xxxii.). The latter part of the tale has been turned into a game for English children, "Mary Brown," given in Miss Plunket's *Merry Games*, but not included in Newell, *Games and Songs of American Children*.

Remarks.—This story is especially interesting as having given rise to a game. Capture and imprisonment are frequently the gruesome *motif* of children's games, as in "Prisoner's base." Here it has been used with romantic effect.

XLVII. MY OWN SELF

Source.—Told to Mrs. Balfour by Mrs. W., a native of North Sunderland, who had seen the cottage and heard the tale from persons who had known the widow and her boy, and had got the story direct from them. The title was "Me A'an Sel'," which I have altered to "My Own Self."

Parallels.—Notwithstanding Mrs. Balfour's informant, the same tale is widely spread in the North Country. Hugh Miller relates it, in his *Scenes from my Childhood*, as "Ainsel"; it is given in Mr. Hartland's *English Folk and Fairy Tales*; Mr. F.B. Jevons has heard it in the neighbourhood of Durham; while a further version appeared in *Monthly Chronicle of North Country Folk-Lore*. Further parallels abroad are enumerated by Mr. Clouston in his *Book of Noodles*, pp. 184-5, and by the late Prof. Köhler in *Orient und Occident*, ii., 331. The expedient by which Ulysses outwits Polyphemus in the Odyssey by calling himself ουτις is clearly of the same order.

Remarks.—The parallel with the Odyssey suggests the possibility that this is the ultimate source of the legend, as other parts of the epic have been adapted to local requirements in Great Britain, as in the "Blinded Giant" (No. lxi.), or "Conall Yellowclaw" (*Celtic Fairy Tales*, No. v.). The fact of Continental parallels disposes of the possibility of its being a merely local legend. The fairies might appear to be in a somewhat novel guise here as something to be afraid of. But this is the usual attitude of the folk towards the "Good People," as indeed their euphemistic name really implies.

XLVIII. THE BLACK BULL OF NORROWAY

Source.—Chambers's *Popular Rhymes of Scotland*, much Anglicised in language, but otherwise unaltered.

Parallels.—Chambers, *l.c.*, gave a variant with the title "The Red Bull o' Norroway." Kennedy, *Legendary Fictions*, p. 87, gives a variant with the title "The Brown Bear of Norway." Mr. Stewart gave a Leitrim version, in which "Norroway" becomes "Orange," in *Folk-Lore* for June, 1893, which Miss Peacock follows up with a Lincolnshire parallel (showing the same corruption of name) in the September number. A reference to the "Black Bull o' Norroway" occurs in Sidney's *Arcadia*, as also in the *Complaynt of Scotland*, 1548. The "sale of bed" incident at the end has been bibliographised by Miss Cox in her volume of variants of *Cinderella*, p. 481. It probably existed in one of the versions of *Nix Nought Nothing* (No. vii.).

Remarks.—The Black Bull is clearly a Beast who ultimately wins a Beauty. But the tale as is told is clearly not sufficiently motivated. Miss Peacock's version renders it likely that a fuller account may yet be recovered in England.

XLIX. YALLERY BROWN

Source.—Mrs. Balfour's "Legends of the Lincolnshire Fens," in *Folk-Lore*, ii. It was told to Mrs. Balfour by a labourer, who professed to be the hero of the story, and related it in the first person. I have given him a name, and changed the narration into the oblique narration, and toned down the dialect.

Parallels.—"Tiddy Mun," the hero of another of Mrs. Balfour's legends (*l.c.*, p. 151) was "none bigger 'n a three years old bairn," and had no proper name.

Remarks.—One might almost suspect Mrs. Balfour of being the victim of a piece of invention on the part of her autobiographical informant. But the scrap of verse, especially in its original dialect, has such a folkish ring that it is probable he was only adapting a local legend to his own circumstances.

L. THE THREE FEATHERS

Source.—Collected by Mrs. Gomme from some hop-pickers near Deptford.

Parallels.—The beginning is *à la* Cupid and Psyche, on which Mr. Lang's monograph in the Carabas series is the classic authority. The remainder is an Eastern tale, the peregrinations of which have been studied by Mr. Clouston in his *Pop. Tales and Fictions*, ii., 289, *seq. The Wright's Chaste Wife* is the English *fabliau* on the subject. M.

Bédier, in his recent work on *Les Fabliaux*, pp. 411-13, denies the Eastern origin of the *fabliau*, but in his Indiaphobia M. Bédier is *capable de tout*. In the Indian version the various messengers are sent by the king to test the chastity of a peerless wife of whom he has heard. The incident occurs in some versions of the "Battle of the Birds" story (*Celtic Fairy Tales*, No. xxiv.), and considering the wide spread of this in the British Isles, it was possibly from this source that it came to Deptford.

LI. SIR GAMMER VANS

Source.—Halliwell's *Nursery Rhymes and Tales.*

Parallels.—There is a Yorkshire Lying Tale in Henderson's *Folk-Lore*, first edition, p. 337, a Suffolk one, "Happy Borz'l," in *Suffolk Notes and Queries*, while a similar jingle of inconsequent absurdities, commencing "So he died, and she unluckily married the barber, and a great bear coming up the street popped his head into the window, saying, 'Do you sell any soap'?" is said to have been invented by Charles James Fox to test Sheridan's memory, who repeated it after one hearing. (Others attribute it to Foote.) Similar *Lugenmärchen* are given by the Grimms, and discussed by them in their Notes, Mrs. Hunt's translation, ii., pp. 424, 435, 442, 450, 452, *cf.* Crane, *Ital. Pop. Tales*, p. 263.

Remarks.—The reference to venison warrants, and bows and arrows seems to argue considerable antiquity for this piece of nonsense. The honorific prefix "Sir" may in that case refer to clerkly qualities rather than to knighthood.

LII. TOM HICKATHRIFT

Source.—From the Chap-book, *c.* 1660, in the Pepysian Library, edited for the Villon Society by Mr. G.L. Gomme. Mr. Nutt, who kindly abridged it for me, writes, "Nothing in the shape of incident has been omitted, and there has been no rewriting beyond a phrase here and there rendered necessary by the process of abridgment. But I have in one case altered the sequence of events putting the fight with the giant last."

Parallels.—There are similar adventures of giants in Hunt's Cornish *Drolls*. Sir Francis Palgrave (*Quart. Rev.*, vol. xxi.), and after him, Mr. Gomme, have drawn attention to certain similarities with the Grettir Saga, but they do not extend beyond general resemblances of great strength. Mr. Gomme, however, adds that the cartwheel "plays a not unimportant part in English folk-lore as a representative of old runic faith" (Villon Soc. edition, p. xv.).

Remarks.—Mr. Gomme, in his interesting Introduction, points out several indications of considerable antiquity for the legend, various expressions in the Pepysian Chap-book ("in the marsh of the Isle of Ely," "good ground"), indicating that it could trace back to the sixteenth century. On the other hand, there is evidence of local tradition persisting from that time onward till the present day (Weaver, *Funerall Monuments*, 1631, pp. 866-7; Spelman, *Icenia*, 1640, p. 138; Dugdale, *Imbanking*, 1662 (ed. 1772, p. 244); Blomefield, *Norfolk*, 1808, ix., pp. 79, 80). These refer to a sepulchral monument in Tylney churchyard which had figured on a stone coffin an axle-tree and cart-wheel. The name in these versions of the legend is given as Hickifric, and he is there represented as a village Hampden who withstood the tyranny of the local lord of the manor. Mr. Gomme is inclined to believe, I understand him, that there is a certain amount of evidence for Tom Hickathrift being a historic personality round whom some of the Scandinavian mythical exploits have gathered. I must refer to his admirable Introduction for the ingenious line of reasoning on which he bases these conclusions. Under any circumstances no English child's library of folk-tales can be considered complete that does not present a version of Mr. Hickathrift's exploits.

LIII. THE HEDLEY KOW

Source.—Told to Mrs. Balfour by Mrs. M. of S. Northumberland. Mrs. M.'s mother told the tale as having happened to a person she had known when young: she had herself seen the Hedley Kow twice, once as a donkey and once as a wisp of straw. "Kow" must not be confounded with the more prosaic animal with a "C."

Parallels.—There is a short reference to the Hedley Kow in Henderson, *l.c.*, first edition, pp. 234-5. Our story is shortly referred to thus: "He would present himself to some old dame gathering sticks, in the form of a truss of straw, which she would be sure to take up and carry away. Then it would become so heavy that she would have to lay her burden down, on which the straw would become 'quick,' rise upright and shuffle away before her, till at last it vanished from her sight with a laugh and shout." Some of Robin Goodfellow's pranks are similar to those of the Hedley Kow. The old woman's content with the changes is similar to that of "Mr. Vinegar." An ascending scale of changes has been studied by Prof. Crane, *Italian Popular Tales*, p. 373.

LIV. GOBBORN SEER

Source.—Collected by Mrs. Gomme from an old woman at Deptford. It is to be remarked that "Gobborn Seer" is Irish (Goban Saor = free carpenter), and is the Irish equivalent of Wayland Smith, and occurs in several place names in Ireland.

Parallels.—The essence of the tale occurs in Kennedy, *l.c.*, p. 67, *seq.* Gobborn Seer's daughter was clearly the clever lass who is found in all parts of the Indo-European world. An instance in my *Indian Fairy Tales*, "Why the Fish Laughed" (No. xxiv.). She has been made a special study by Prof. Child, *English and Scotch Ballads*, i., 485, while an elaborate monograph by Prof. Benfey under the title "Die Kluge Dirne" (reprinted in his *Kleine Schriften*, ii., 156, *seq.*), formed the occasion for his first presentation of his now well-known hypothesis of the derivation of all folk-tales from India.

Remarks.—But for the accident of the title being preserved there would have been nothing to show that this tale had been imported into England from Ireland, whither it had probably been carried all the way from India.

LV. LAWKAMERCYME

Source.—Halliwell, *Nursery Rhymes*.

Parallels.—It is possible that this is an Eastern "sell": it occurs at any rate as the first episode in Fitzgerald's translation of Jami's *Salámán and Absál*. Jami, *ob*. 1492, introduces the story to illustrate the perplexities of the problem of individuality in a pantheistic system.

Lest, like the simple Arab in the tale,
I grow perplext, O God! 'twixt ME and THEE,
If I—this Spirit that inspires me whence?
If THOU—then what this sensual impotence?

In other words, M. Bourget's *Cruelle Enigme*. The Arab yokel coming to Bagdad is fearful of losing his identity, and ties a pumpkin to his leg before going to sleep. His companion transfers it to his own leg. The yokel awaking is perplexed like the pantheist.

If I—the pumpkin why on YOU?
If YOU—then where am I, and WHO?

LVI. TATTERCOATS

Source.—Told to Mrs. Balfour by a little girl named Sally Brown, when she lived in the Cars in Lincolnshire. Sally had got it from her mother, who worked for Mrs. Balfour. It was originally told in dialect, which Mrs. Balfour has omitted.

Parallels.—Miss Cox has included "Tattercoats" in her exhaustive collection of parallels of *Cinderella* (Folk-Lore Society Publications, 1892), No. 274 from the MS. which I had lent her. Miss Cox rightly classes it as "Indeterminate," and it has only the *Menial Heroine* and *Happy Marriage* episodes in common with stories of the Cinderella type.

Remarks.—*Tattercoats* is of interest chiefly as being without any "fairy" or supernatural elements, unless the magic pipe can be so considered; it certainly gives the tale a fairy-like element. It is practically a prose variant of *King Cophetua and the Beggar Maid*, and is thus an instance of the folk-novel pure and simple, without any admixture of those unnatural incidents which transform the folk-novel into the serious folk-tale as we are accustomed to have it. Which is the prior, folk-novel or tale, it would be hard to say.

LVII. THE WEE BANNOCK

Source.—Chambers's *Popular Rhymes of Scotland*. I have attempted an impossibility, I fear, in trying to anglicise, but the fun of the original tempted me. There still remain several technical trade terms requiring elucidation. I owe the following to the kindness of the Rev. Mr. Todd Martin, of Belfast. *Lawtrod* = lap board on which the tailor irons; *tow cards*, the comb with which tow is carded; the *clove*, a heavy wooden knife for breaking up the flax. *Heckling* is combing it with a *heckle* or wooden comb; *binnings* are halters for cattle made of *sprit* or rushes. *Spurtle* = spoon; *whins* = gorse.

Parallels.—This is clearly a variant of *Johnny-cake* = journey-cake, No. xxviii., where see Notes.

Remarks.—But here the interest is with the pursuers rather than with the pursued. The subtle characterisation of the various occupations reaches a high level of artistic merit. Mr. Barrie himself could scarcely have succeeded better in a very difficult task.

LVIII. JOHNNY GLOKE

Source.—Contributed by Mr. W. Gregor to *Folk-Lore Journal*, vii. I have rechristened "Johnny Glaik" for the sake of the rhyme, and anglicised the few Scotticisms.

Parallels.—This is clearly *The Valiant Tailor* of the Grimms: "x at a blow" has been bibliographised. (See my List of Incidents in Trans. Folk-Lore Congress, 1892, *sub voce*.)

Remarks.—How *The Valiant Tailor* got to Aberdeen one cannot tell, though the resemblance is close enough to suggest a direct "lifting" from some English version of Grimm's *Goblins*. At the same time it must be remembered that *Jack the Giant Killer* (see Notes on No. xix.) contains some of the incidents of *The Valiant Tailor*.

LIX. COAT O CLAY

Source.—Contributed by Mrs. Balfour originally to *Longman's Magazine*, and thence to *Folk-Lore*, Sept., 1890.

Remarks.—A rustic apologue, which is scarcely more than a prolonged pun on "Coat o' Clay." Mrs. Balfour's telling redeems it from the usual dulness of folk-tales with a moral or a double meaning.

LX. THE THREE COWS

Source.—Contributed to Henderson, *l.c.*, pp. 321-2, by the Rev. S. Baring-Gould.

Parallels.—The incident "Bones together" occurs in *Rushen Coatie* (*infra*, No. lxx.), and has been discussed by the Grimms, i., 399, and by Prof. Köhler, *Or. und Occ.*, ii., 680.

LXI. THE BLINDED GIANT

Source.—Henderson's *Folk-Lore of Northern Counties*. See also *Folk-Lore*.

Parallels.—Polyphemus in the Odyssey and the Celtic parallels in *Celtic Fairy Tales*, No. v., "Conall Yellowclaw." The same incident occurs in one of Sindbad's voyages.

Remarks.—Here we have another instance of the localisation of a well-known myth. There can be little doubt that the version is ultimately to be traced back to the Odyssey.

The one-eyed giant, the barred door, the escape through the blinded giant's legs in the skin of a slaughtered animal, are a series of incidents that could not have arisen independently and casually. Yet till lately the mill stood to prove if the narrator lied, and every circumstance of local particularity seemed to vouch for the autochthonous character of the myth. The incident is an instructive one, and I have therefore included it in this volume, though it is little more than an anecdote in its present shape.

LXII. SCRAPEFOOT

Source.—Collected by Mr. Batten from Mrs. H., who heard it from her mother over forty years ago.

Parallels.—It is clearly a variant of Southey's *Three Bears* (No. xviii.).

Remarks.—This remarkable variant raises the question whether Southey did anything more than transform Scrapefoot into his naughty old woman, who in her turn has been transformed by popular tradition into the naughty girl Silver-hair. Mr. Nutt ingeniously suggests that Southey heard the story told of an old vixen, and mistook the rustic name of a female fox for the metaphorical application to women of fox-like temper. Mrs. H.'s version to my mind has all the marks of priority. It is throughout an animal tale, the touch at the end of the shaking the paws and the name Scrapefoot are too *volkstümlich* to have been conscious variations on Southey's tale. In introducing the story in his *Doctor*, the poet laureate did not claim to do more than repeat a popular tale. I think that there can be little doubt that in Mrs. H.'s version we have now recovered this in its original form. If this is so, we may here have one more incident of the great Northern beast epic of bear and fox, on which Prof. Krohn has written an instructive monograph, *Bär (Wolf.) und Fuchs* (Helsingfors, 1889).

LXIII. THE PEDLAR OF SWAFFHAM

Source.—*Diary of Abraham de la Pryme* (Surtees Soc.) under date 10th November, 1699, but rewritten by Mr. Nutt, who has retained the few characteristic seventeenth century touches of Pryme's dull and colourless narration. There is a somewhat fuller account in Blomefield's *History of Norfolk*, vi., 211-13, from Twysden's *Reminiscences*, ed. Hearne, p. 299, in this there is a double treasure; the first in an iron pot with a Latin inscription, which the pedlar, whose name is John Chapman, does not understand. Inquiring its meaning from a learned friend, he is told—

Under me doth lie
Another much richer than I.

He accordingly digs deeper and finds another pot of gold.

Parallels.—Blomefield refers to Fungerus, *Etymologicum Latino-Græcum*, pp. 1110-11, where the same story is told of a peasant of Dort, in Holland, who was similarly directed to go to Kempen Bridge. Prof. E.B. Cowell, who gives the passage from Fungerus in a special paper on the subject in the *Journal of Philology*, vi., 189-95, points out that the same story occurs in the *Masnávi* of the Persian port Jalaluddin, whose *floruit* is 1260 A.D. Here a young spendthrift of Bagdad is warned in a dream to repair to Cairo, with the usual result of being referred back.

Remarks.—The artificial character of the incident is sufficient to prevent its having occurred in reality or to more than one inventive imagination. It must therefore have been brought to Europe from the East and adapted to local conditions at Dort and Swaffham. Prof. Cowell suggests that it was possibly adapted at the latter place to account for the effigy of the pedlar and his dog.

LXIV. THE OLD WITCH

Source.—Collected by Mrs. Gomme at Deptford.

Parallels.—I have a dim memory of hearing a similar tale in Australia in 1860. It is clearly parallel with the Grimms' *Frau Holle*, where the good girl is rewarded and the bad punished in a similar way. Perrault's *Toads and Diamonds* is of the same *genus*.

LXV. THE THREE WISHES

Source.—Steinberg's *Folk-Lore of Northamptonshire*, 1851, but entirely rewritten by Mr. Nutt, who has introduced from other variants one touch at the close—viz., the readiness of the wife to allow her husband to remain disfigured.

Parallels.—Perrault's *Trois Souhaits* is the same tale, and Mr. Lang has shown in his edition of Perrault (pp. xlii.-li.) how widely spread is the theme throughout the climes and the ages. I do not, however, understand him to grant that they are all derived from one source—that represented in the Indian *Pantschatantra*. In my *Æsop*, i., 140-1, I have pointed out an earlier version in Phædrus where it occurs (as in the prose versions) as the fable of *Mercury and the two Women*, one of whom wishes to see her babe when it has a beard; the other, that everything she touches which she would find useful in her profession, may follow her. The babe becomes bearded, and the other woman raising her hand to wipe her eyes finds her nose following her hand—*dénouement* on which the scene closes. M. Bédier, as usual, denies the Indian origin, *Les Fabliaux*, pp. 177, *seq*.

Remarks.—I have endeavoured to show, *l.c.*, that the Phædrine form is ultimately to be derived from India, and there can be little doubt that all the other variants, which are only variations on one idea, and that an absurdly incongruous one, were derived from India in the last resort. The case is strongest for drolls of this kind.

LXVI. THE BURIED MOON

Source.—Mrs. Balfour's "Legends of the Lincolnshire Cars" in *Folk-Lore*, ii., somewhat abridged and the dialect removed. The story was derived from a little girl named Bratton, who declared she had heard it from her "grannie." Mrs. Balfour thinks the girl's own weird imagination had much to do with framing the details.

Remarks.—The tale is noteworthy as being distinctly mythical in character, and yet collected within the last ten years from one of the English peasantry. The conception of the moon as a beneficent being, the natural enemy of the bogles and other dwellers of the dark, is natural enough, but scarcely occurs, so far as I recollect, in other mythological systems. There is, at any rate, nothing analogous in the Grimms' treatment of the moon in their *Teutonic Mythology*, tr. Stallybrass, pp. 701-21.

LXVII. A SON OF ADAM

Source.—From memory, by Mr. E. Sidney Hartland, as heard by him from his nurse in childhood.

Parallels.—Jacques de Vitry *Exempla*, ed. Prof. Crane, No. xiii., and references given in notes, p. 139. It occurs in Swift and in modern Italian folk-lore.

Remarks.—The *Exempla* were anecdotes, witty and otherwise, used by the monks in their sermons to season their discourse. Often they must have been derived from the folk of the period, and at first sight it might seem that we had found still extant among the folk the story that had been the original of Jacques de Vitry's *Exemplum*. But the theological basis of the story shows clearly that it was originally a monkish invention and came thence among the folk.

LXVIII. THE CHILDREN IN THE WOOD

Source.—Percy, *Reliques*. The ballad form of the story has become such a nursery classic that I had not the heart to "prose" it. As Mr. Allingham remarks, it is the best of the ballads of the pedestrian order.

Parallels.—The second of R. Yarrington's *Two Lamentable Tragedies*, 1601, has the same plot as the ballad. Several chap-books have been made out of it, some of them enumerated by Halliwell's *Popular Histories* (Percy Soc.) No. 18. From one of these I am in the fortunate position of giving the names of the *dramatis personæ* of this domestic tragedy. Androgus was the wicked uncle, Pisaurus his brother who married Eugenia, and their children in the wood were Cassander and little Kate. The ruffians were appropriately named Rawbones and Woudkill. According to a writer in *3 Notes and Queries*, ix., 144, the traditional burial-place of the children is pointed out in Norfolk. The ballad was known before Percy, as it is mentioned in the *Spectator*, Nos. 80 and 179.

Remarks.—The only "fairy" touch—but what a touch!—the pall of leaves collected by the robins.

LXIX. THE HOBYAHS

Source.—*American Folk-Lore Journal*, iii., 173, contributed by Mr. S.V. Proudfit as current in a family deriving from Perth.

Remarks.—But for the assurance of the tale itself that Hobyahs are no more, Mr. Batten's portraits of them would have convinced me that they were the bogles or spirits of the comma bacillus. Mr. Proudfit remarks that the cry "Look me" was very impressive.

LXX. A POTTLE O' BRAINS

Source.—Contributed by Mrs. Balfour to *Folk-Lore*, II.

Parallels.—The fool's wife is clearly related to the Clever Lass of "Gobborn Seer," where see Notes.

Remarks.—The fool is obviously of the same family as he of the "Coat o' Clay" (No. lix.) if he is not actually identical with him. His adventures might be regarded as a sequel to the former ones. The Noodle family is strongly represented in English folk-tales, which would seem to confirm Carlyle's celebrated statistical remark.

LXXI. THE KING OF ENGLAND

Source.—Mr. F. Hindes Groome, *In Gypsy Tents*, told him by John Roberts, a Welsh gypsy, with a few slight changes and omission of passages insisting upon the gypsy origin of the three helpful brothers.

Parallels.—The king and his three sons are familiar figures in European *märchen*. Slavonic parallels are enumerated by Leskien Brugman in their *Lithauische Märchen*, notes on No. 11, p. 542. The Sleeping Beauty is of course found in Perrault.

Remarks.—The tale is scarcely a good example for Mr. Hindes Groome's contention (in *Transactions Folk-Lore Congress*) for the diffusion of all folk-tales by means of gypsies as *colporteurs*. This is merely a matter of evidence, and of evidence there is singularly little, though it is indeed curious that one of Campbell's best equipped informants should turn out to be a gypsy. Even this fact, however, is not too well substantiated.

LXXII. KING JOHN AND THE ABBOT

Source.—"Prosed" from the well-known ballad in Percy. I have changed the first query: What am I worth? Answer: Twenty-nine pence—one less, I ween, than the Lord. This would have sounded somewhat bold in prose.

Parallels.—Vincent of Beauvais has the story, but the English version comes from the German Joe Miller, Pauli's *Schimpf und Ernst*, No. lv., p. 46, ed. Oesterley, where see his notes. The question I have omitted exists there, and cannot have "independently arisen." Pauli was a fifteenth century worthy or unworthy.

Remarks.—Riddles were once on a time serious things to meddle with, as witness Samson and the Sphynx, and other instances duly noted with his customary erudition by Prof. Child in his comments on the ballad, *English and Scotch Ballads*, i, 403-14.

LXXIII. RUSHEN COATIE

Source.—I have concocted this English, or rather Scotch, Cinderella from the various versions given in Miss Cox's remarkable collection of 345 variants of *Cinderella* (Folk-Lore Society, 1892); see *Parallels* for an enumeration of those occurring in the British Isles. I have used Nos. 1-3, 8-10. I give my composite the title "Rushen Coatie," to differentiate it from any of the Scotch variants, and for the purposes of a folk-lore experiment. If this book becomes generally used among English-speaking peoples, it may possibly re-introduce this and other tales among the folk. We should be able to trace this re-introduction by the variation in titles. I have done the same with "Nix Nought Nothing," "Molly Whuppie," and "Johnny Gloke."

Parallels.—Miss Cox's volume gives no less than 113 variants of the pure type of Cinderella—her type A. "Cinderella, or the Fortunate Marriage of a Despised Scullery-maid by Aid of an *Animal* God-mother through the Test of a Slipper"—such might be the explanatory title of a chap-book dealing with the pure type of Cinderella. This is represented in Miss Cox's book, so far as the British Isles are concerned, by no less than seven variants, as follows: (1) Dr. Blind, in *Archæological Review*, iii., 24-7, "Ashpitell" (from neighbourhood of Glasgow). (2) A. Lang, in *Revue Celtique*, t. iii., reprinted in *Folk-Lore*, September, 1890, "Rashin Coatie" (from Morayshire). (3) Mr. Gregor, in *Folk-Lore Journal*, ii., 72-4 (from Aberdeenshire), "The Red Calf"—all these in Lowland Scots. (4) Campbell, *Popular Tales*, No. xliii., ii., 286 *seq.*, "The Sharp Grey Sheep." (5) Mr. Sinclair, in *Celtic Mag.*, xiii., 454-65, "Snow-white Maiden." (6) Mr. Macleod's variant communicated through Mr. Nutt to Miss Cox's volume, p. 533; and (7) Curtin, *Myths of Ireland*, pp. 78-92. "Fair, Brown, and Trembling"—these four in Gaelic, the last in Erse. To these I would add (8, 9) Chambers's two versions in *Pop. Rhymes of Scotland*, pp. 66-8, "Rashie Coat," though Miss Cox assimilates them to Type B. Catskin; and (10) a variant of Dr. Blind's version, unknown to Miss Cox, but given in 7 *Notes and Queries*, x., 463 (Dumbartonshire). Mr. Clouston has remarks on the raven as omen-bird in his notes to Mrs. Saxby's *Birds of Omen in Shetland* (privately printed, 1893).

ENGLISH VARIANTS OF CINDERELLA

GREGOR.	LANG.	CHAMBERS, I. and II.	BLIND.
Ill-treated heroine (by parents).	Calf given by dying mother.	*Heroine dislikes husband.*	Ill-treated heroine (by step-mother).
Helpful animal (red calf).	Ill-treated heroine (by stepmother and sisters).	*Henwife aid.*	Menial heroine.
Spy on heroine.	Heroine disguise (rashin coatie).	*Countertasks.*	Helpful animal (black sheep).
Slaying of helpful animal threatened.	Hearth abode.	*Heroine disguise.*	Ear cornucopia.
Heroine flight.	Helpful animal.	*Heroine flight.*	Spy on heroine.
Heroine disguise (rashin coatie).	Slaying of helpful animal.	Menial heroine.	Slaying of helpful animal.
Menial heroine.	Revivified bones.	(Fairy) aid.	Old woman advice.
	Help at grave.		Revivified bones.
	Dinner cooked (by helpful animal).		Task performing animal.
Magic dresses (given by calf).	Magic dresses.	Magic dresses.	Meeting-place (church).
Meeting-place (church).	Meeting-place (church).	Meeting-place (church).	Dresses (not magic).
Flight.	Flight threefold.	Flight threefold.	Flight twofold.
Lost shoe.	Lost shoe.	Lost shoe.	Lost shoe.
Shoe marriage test.	Shoe marriage test.	Shoe marriage test.	Shoe marriage test.
Mutilated foot (housewife's daughter).	Mutilated foot.	Mutilated foot.	Mutilated foot
Bird witness.	False bride.	False bride.	False bride.
Happy marriage.	Bird witness.	Bird witness.	Bird witness (raven).
House for red	Happy	Happy marriage.	Happy

| calf. | marriage. | | marriage. |

Remarks.—In going over these various versions, the first and perhaps most striking thing that comes out is the substantial agreement of the variants in each *language*. The English—*i.e.*, Scotch, variants go together; the Gaelic ones agree to differ from the English. I can best display this important agreement and difference by the accompanying two tables, which give, in parallel columns, Miss Cox's abstracts of her tabulations, in which each incident is shortly given in technical phraseology. It is practically impossible to use the long tabulations for comparative purposes without some such shorthand.

CELTIC VARIANTS OF CINDERELLA

MACLEOD.	CAMPBELL.	SINCLAIR.	CURTIN.
Heroine, daughter of sheep, king's wife.	Ill-treated heroine (by stepmother).	Ill-treated heroine (by stepmother and sisters).	Ill-treated heroine (by elder sisters).
	Menial heroine.	Menial heroine.	Menial heroine.
	Helpful animal.	Helpful cantrips.	Henwife aid.
Spy on heroine.	Spy on heroine.	Magic dresses (+ starlings on shoulders).	Magic dresses (honey-bird finger and stud).
Eye sleep threefold.	Eye sleep.	Meeting-place (church).	Meeting place (church).
Slaying of helpful animal mother.	Slaying of helpful animal.	Flight twofold.	Flight threefold.
Revivified bones.	Revivified bones.	Lost shoe.	Lost shoe.
Magic dresses.	Step-sister substitute.	Shoe marriage test.	Shoe marriage test.
	Golden shoe gift (from hero).	Heroine under washtub.	Mutilated foot.
Meeting-place (feast).	Meeting-place (sermon).	Happy marriage.	Happy marriage.
Flight threefold.	Flight threefold.	Substituted bride.	Substituted bride (eldest sister).
Lost shoe (golden).	Lost shoe.	Jonah heroine.	Jonah heroine.
Shoe marriage test.	Shoe marriage test.	Three reappearances.	Three reappearances.
Mutilated foot.	Mutilated foot.	Reunion.	Reunion.
	False bride.		Villain Nemesis.
Bird witness.	Bird witness.		
Happy marriage.	Happy marriage.		

Now, in the "English" versions there is practical unanimity in the concluding portions of the tale. *Magic dresses—Meeting-place (Church)—Flight—Lost Shoe—Shoe Marriage-test—Mutilated foot—False Bride—Bird witness—Happy Marriage*, follow one another with exemplary regularity in all four (six) versions.[2] The introductory incidents vary somewhat. Chambers has evidently a maimed version of the introduction of Catskin (see No. lxxxiii.). The remaining three enable us, however, to restore with some confidence the *Ur*-Cinderella in English somewhat as follows: *Helpful animal given by dying mother—Ill-treated heroine—Menial heroine—cornucopia—Spy on heroine—Slaying by helpful animal—Tasks—Revivified bones*. I have attempted in my version to reconstruct the "English" Cinderella according to these formulæ. It will be observed that the helpful animal is helpful in two ways (a) in helping the heroine to perform tasks; (b) in providing her with magic dresses. It is the same with the Grimms' *Aschenputtel* and other Continental variants.

Turning to the Celtic variants, these divide into two sets. Campbell's and Macleod's versions are practically at one with the English formula, the latter with an important variation which will concern us later. But the other two, Curtin's and Sinclair's, one collected in Ireland and the other in Scotland, both continue the formula with the conclusion of the Sea Maiden tale (on which see the Notes of my *Celtic Fairy Tales*, No. xvii.). This is a specifically Celtic formula, and would seem therefore to claim Cinderella for the Celts. But the welding of the Sea Maiden ending on to the Cinderella formula is clearly a later and inartistic junction, and implies rather imperfect assimilation of the Cinderella formula. To determine the question of origin we must turn to the purer type given by the other two Celtic versions.

Campbell's tale can clearly lay no claim to represent the original type of Cinderella. The golden shoes are a gift of the hero to the heroine which destroys the whole point of the *Shoe marriage test*, and cannot have been in the original, wherever it originated. Mr. Macleod's version, however, contains an incident which seems to bring us nearer to the original form than any version contained in Miss Cox's book. Throughout the variants it will be observed what an important function is played by the helpful animal. This in some of the versions is left as a legacy by the heroine's dying mother. But in Mr. Macleod's version the helpful animal, a sheep, is the heroine's mother herself! This is indeed an archaic touch, which seems to hark back to primitive times and totemistic beliefs. And more important still, it is a touch which vitalises the other variants in which the helpful animal is rather dragged in by the horns. Mr. Nutt's lucky find at the last moment seems to throw more light on the origin of the tale than almost the whole of the remaining collection.

But does this find necessarily prove an original Celtic origin for Cinderella? Scarcely. It remains to be proved that this introductory part of the story with helpful animal was necessarily part of the original. Having regard to the feudal character underlying the whole conception, it remains possible that the earlier part was ingeniously dovetailed on to the latter from some pre-existing and more archaic tale, perhaps that represented by the Grimms' *One Eyed, Two Eyes, and Three Eyes*. The possibility of the introduction of an archaic formula which had become a convention of folk-telling cannot be left out of account.

The "Youngest-best" formula which occurs in Cinderella, and on which Mr. Lang laid much stress in his treatment of the subject in his "Perrault" as a survival of the old tenure of "junior right," does not throw much light on the subject. Mr. Ralston, in the *Nineteenth Century*, 1879, was equally unenlightening with his sun-myths.

[2]

Chamber's II. consists entirely and solely of these incidents.

LXXIV. KING O' CATS

Source.—I have taken a point here and a point there from the various English versions mentioned in the next section.

I have expanded the names, so as to make a jingle from the Dildrum and Doldrum of Hartland.

Parallels.—Five variants of this quaint legend have been collected in England: (1) Halliwell, *Pop. Rhymes*, 167, "Molly Dixon"; (2) *Choice Notes—Folk-Lore*, p. 73, "Colman Grey"; (3) *Folk-Lore Journal*, ii., 22, "King o' the Cats"; (4) *Folk-Lore—England* (Gibbings), "Johnny Reed's Cat"; (5) Hartland and Wilkinson, *Lancashire Legends*, p. 13, "Dildrum Doldrum." Sir F. Palgrave gives a Danish parallel; *cf.* Halliwell, *l.c.*

Remarks.—An interesting example of the spread and development of a simple anecdote throughout England. Here again we can scarcely imagine more than a single origin for the tale which is, in its way, as weird and fantastic as E.A. Poe.

LXXV. TAMLANE

Source.—From Scott's *Minstrelsy*, with touches from the other variants given by Prof. Child in his *Eng. and Scotch Ballads*, i., 335-58.

Parallels.—Prof. Child gives no less than nine versions in his masterly edition, *l.c.*, besides another fragment "Burd Ellen and Young Tamlane," i., 258. He parallels the marriage of Peleus and Thetis in Apollodorus III., xiii., 5, 6, which still persists in modern Greece as a Cretan ballad.

Remarks.—Prof. Child remarks that dipping into water or milk is necessary before transformation can take place, and gives examples, *l.c.*, 338, to which may be added that of Catskin (see Notes *infra*). He gives as the reason why the Elf-queen would have "ta'en out Tamlane's two grey eyne," so that henceforth he should not be able to see the fairies. Was it not rather that he should not henceforth see Burd Janet?—a subtle touch of jealousy. On dwelling in fairyland Mr. Hartland has a monograph in his *Science of Fairy Tales*, pp. 161-254.

LXXVI. THE STARS IN THE SKY

Source.—Mrs. Balfour's old nurse, now in New Zealand. The original is in broad Scots, which I have anglicised.

Parallels.—The tradition is widespread that at the foot of the rainbow treasure is to be found; *cf.* Mr. John Payne's "Sir Edward's Questing" in his *Songs of Life and Death*.

Remarks.—The "sell" at the end is scarcely after the manner of the folk, and various touches throughout indicate a transmission through minds tainted with culture and introspection.

LXXVII. NEWS!

Source.—Bell's *Speaker*.

Parallels.—Jacques de Vitry, *Exempla*, ed. Crane, No. ccv., a servant being asked the news by his master returned from a pilgrimage to Compostella, says the dog is lame, and goes on to explain: "While the dog was running near the mule, the mule kicked him and broke his own halter and ran through the house, scattering the fire with his hoofs, and burning down your house with your wife." It occurs even earlier in Alfonsi's *Disciplina Clericalis*, No. xxx., at beginning of the twelfth century, among the *Fabliaux*, and in Bebel, *Werke*, iii., 71, whence probably it was reintroduced into England. See Prof. Crane's note *ad loc.*

Remarks.—Almost all Alfonsi's *exempla* are from the East. It is characteristic that the German version finishes up with a loss of honour, the English climax being loss of fortune.

LXXVIII. PUDDOCK, MOUSIE, AND RATTON

Source.—Kirkpatrick Sharpe's *Ballad Book*, 1824, slightly anglicised.

Parallels.—Mr. Bullen, in his *Lyrics from Elizabethan Song Books*, p. 202, gives a version, "The Marriage of the Frog and the Mouse," from T. Ravenscroft's *Melismata*, 1611. The nursery rhyme of the frog who would a-wooing go is clearly a variant of this, and has thus a sure pedigree of three hundred years; *cf.* "Frog husband" in my List of Incidents, or notes to "The Well of the World's End" (No. xli.).

LXXIX. LITTLE BULL-CALF

Source.—*Gypsy Lore Journal*, iii., one of a number of tales told "In a Tent" to Mr. John Sampson. I have respelt and euphemised the bladder.

Parallels.—The Perseus and Andromeda incident is frequent in folk-tales; see my List of Incidents *sub voce* "Fight with Dragon." "Cheese squeezing," as a test of prowess, is also common, as in "Jack the Giant Killer" and elsewhere (Köhler, *Jahrbuch*, vii., 252).

LXXX. THE WEE WEE MANNIE

Source.—From Mrs. Balfour's old nurse. I have again anglicised.

Parallels.—This is one of the class of accumulative stories like *The Old Woman and her Pig* (No. iv.). The class is well represented in these isles.

LXXXI. HABETROT AND SCANTLIE MAB

Source.—Henderson's *Folk-Lore of Northern Counties*, pp. 258-62 of Folk-Lore Society's edition. I have abridged and to some extent rewritten.

Parallels.—This in its early part is a parallel to the *Tom Tit Tot*, which see. The latter part is more novel, and is best compared with the Grimms' *Spinners*.

Remark.—Henderson makes out of Habetrot a goddess of the spinning-wheel, but with very little authority as it seems to me.

LXXXII. OLD MOTHER WIGGLE WAGGLE

Source.—I have inserted into Halliwell's version one current in Mr. Batten's family, except that I have substituted "Wiggle-Waggle" for "Slipper-Slopper." The two versions supplement one another.

Remarks.—This is a pure bit of animal satire, which might have come from a rural Jefferies with somewhat more of wit than the native writer.

LXXXIII. CATSKIN

Source.—From the chap-book reprinted in Halliwell I have introduced the demand for magic dresses from Chambers's *Rashie Coat*, into which it had clearly been interpolated from some version of Catskin.

Parallels.—Miss Cox's admirable volume of variants of *Cinderella* also contains seventy-three variants of *Catskin*, besides thirteen "indeterminate" ones which approximate to that type. Of these eighty-six, five exist in the British Isles, two chap-books given in Halliwell and in Dixon's *Songs of English Peasantry*, two by Campbell, Nos. xiv. and xiv*a*, "The King who Wished to Marry his Daughter," and one by Kennedy's *Fireside Stories*, "The Princess in the Catskins." Goldsmith knew the story by the name of "Catskin," as he refers to it in the *Vicar*. There is a fragment from Cornwall in *Folk-Lore*, i., App. p. 149.

Remarks.—Catskin, or the Wandering Gentlewomen, now exists in English only in two chap-book ballads. But Chambers's first variant of *Rashie Coat* begins with the Catskin formula in a euphemised form. The full formula may be said to run in abbreviated form—*Death-bed promise—Deceased wife's resemblance marriage test—Unnatural father* (desiring to marry his own daughter)—*Helpful animal—Counter tasks—Magic dresses—Heroine flight—Heroine disguise—Menial heroine—Meeting-place—Token objects named—Threefold flight—Lovesick prince—Recognition ring—Happy marriage*. Of these the chap-book versions contain scarcely anything of the opening *motifs*. Yet they existed in England, for Miss Isabella Barclay, in a variant which Miss Cox has overlooked (*Folk-Lore*, i., *l.c.*), remembers having heard the Unnatural Father incident from a Cornish servant-girl. Campbell's two versions also contain the incident, from which one of them receives its name. One wonders in what form Mr. Burchell knew Catskin, for "he gave the [Primrose] children the Buck of Beverland,[3] with the history of Patient Grissel, the adventures of Catskin and the Fair Rosamond's Bower" (*Vicar of Wakefield*, 1766, c. vi.). Pity that "Goldy" did not tell the story himself, as he had probably heard it in Ireland, where Kennedy gives a poor version in his *Fireside Stories*.

Yet, imperfect as the chap-book versions are, they yet retain not a few archaic touches. It is clear from them, at any rate, that the Heroine was at one time transformed into a Cat. For when the basin of water is thrown in her face she "shakes her ears" just as a cat would. Again, before putting on her magic dresses she bathes in a pellucid pool. Now, Professor Child has pointed out in his notes on Tamlane and elsewhere (*English and Scotch Ballads*, i., 338; ii., 505; iii., 505) that dipping into water or milk is necessary before transformation can take place. It is clear, therefore, that Catskin was originally transformed into an animal by the spirit of her mother, also transformed into an animal.

If I understand Mr. Nutt rightly (*Folk-Lore*, iv, 135, *seq.*), he is inclined to think, from the evidence of the hero-tales which have the unsavoury *motif* of the Unnatural Father, that the original home of the story was England, where most of the hero-tales locate the incident. I would merely remark on this that there are only very slight traces of the story in these islands nowadays, while it abounds in Italy, which possesses one almost perfect version of the formula (Miss Cox, No. 142, from Sardinia).

Mr. Newell, on the other hand (*American Folk-Lore Journal*, ii., 160), considers Catskin the earliest of the three types contained in Miss Cox's book, and considers that Cinderella was derived from this as a softening of the original. His chief reason appears to be the earlier appearance of Catskin in Straparola,[4] 1550, a hundred years earlier than Cinderella in Basile, 1636. This appears to be a somewhat insufficient basis for such a conclusion. Nor is there, after all, so close a relation between the two types in their full development as to necessitate the derivation of one from the other.

[3]

Who knows the Buck of Beverland nowadays?

[4]

It is practically in Des Perier's *Récréations*, 1544.

LXXXIV. STUPID'S CRIES

Source.—*Folk-Lore Record*, iii., 152-5, by the veteran Prof. Stephens. I have changed "dog and bitch" of original to "dog and cat," and euphemised the liver and lights.

Parallels.—Prof. Stephens gives parallels from Denmark. Germany (the Grimms' *Up Riesensohn*) and Ireland (Kennedy, *Fireside Stories*, p. 30).

LXXXV. THE LAMBTON WORM

Source.—Henderson's *Folk-Lore of Northern Counties*, pp. 287-9, I have rewritten, as the original was rather high falutin'.

Parallels.—Worms or dragons form the subject of the whole of the eighth chapter of Henderson. "The Laidly Worm of Spindleston Heugh" (No. xxxiii.) also requires the milk of nine kye for its daily rations, and cow's milk is the ordinary provender of such kittle cattle (Grimms' *Teut. Myth.* 687), the mythological explanation being that cows = the clouds and the dragon = the storm. Jephtha vows are also frequent in folk-tales: Miss Cox gives many examples in her *Cinderella*, p. 511.

Remarks.—Nine generations back from the last of the Lambtons, Henry Lambton, M.P., ob. 1761, reaches Sir John Lambton, Knight of Rhodes, and several instances of violent death occur in the interim. Dragons are possibly survivals into historic times of antedeluvian monsters, or reminiscences of classical legend (Perseus, etc.). Who shall say which is which, as Mr. Lang would observe.

LXXXVI. WISE MEN OF GOTHAM

Source.—The chap-book contained in Mr. Hazlitt's *Shaksperian Jest Book*, vol. iii. I have selected the incidents and modernised the spelling; otherwise the droll remains as it was told in Elizabethan times.

Parallels.—Mr. Clouston's *Book of Noodles* is little else than a series of parallels to our droll. See my List of Incidents under the titles, "One cheese after another," "Hare postman," "Not counting self," "Drowning eels." In most cases Mr. Clouston quotes Eastern analogies.

Remarks.—All countries have their special crop of fools, Boeotians among the Greeks, the people of Hums among the Persians (how appropriate!), the Schildburgers in Germany, and so on. Gotham is the English representative, and as witticisms call to mind well-known wits, so Gotham has had heaped on its head all the stupidities of the Indo-

European world. For there can be little doubt that these drolls have spread from East to West. This "Not counting self" is in the *Gooroo Paramastan*, the cheeses "one after another" in M. Rivière's collection of Kabyle tales, and so on. It is indeed curious how little originality there is among mankind in the matter of stupidity. Even such an inventive genius as the late Mr. Sothern had considerable difficulty in inventing a new "sell."

LXXXVII. PRINCESS OF CANTERBURY

Source.—I have inserted into the old chap-book version of the *Four Kings of Colchester, Canterbury*, &c., an incident entitled by Halliwell "The Three Questions."

Parallels.—The "riddle bride wager" is a frequent incident of folk-tales (see my List of Incidents); the sleeping tabu of the latter part is not so common, though it occurs, *e.g.*, in the Grimms' *Twelve Princesses*, who wear out their shoes with dancing.

Printed in Great Britain
by Amazon